OBSCURA

an urban fantasy
anthology

Cover design: Michelle Schad
Interior design: Karen Garvin

ISBN 978-1-950903-10-8

CONTENTS

The Druid of Market Street 7
  Sean Hillman

Skin Deep 23
  L. N. Hunter

The Working of Wax 39
  Jen Sexton-Riley

Changing Gabe 57
  Kathrine Stewart

Like the Bright Moon 69
  Kelsey Wheaton

Lucifer's Lights 97
  Karen Garvin

Periodic Magic 133
  Cathryn Leigh

Skinwalkers 173
  Michelle Schad

About the Authors 202

THE DRUID
OF MARKET STREET

Sean Hillman

Atlanta in July is a broiler that can reduce a man to a puddle of human flesh, prostrate on the nearest cool, flat surface. Even in the morning, the air is thick and in the heart of the city the only wind is from passing engines designed to make the air thicker. It can drive you mad, if you let it. But this city is my home, has been for fifty years, and I am not about to give her up, even if the summers are hotter and longer with each passing year.

This morning starts like all my mornings...

Hold up, I don't want to start lying to you right off the bat. No, that would get us off on the wrong foot. All my mornings do not start like this morning did, only some of them. Please allow me to amend my statement before we go on.

This morning starts off like a lot of my mornings (better, yes, much better) with me sitting out in front of my flower shop, reading the sports page. I am running down the at-bats for the Braves last night, not bothering to look at the pitching stats. I was at the game, of course, and know how we lost it in ten innings, but I like to look anyway. Sometimes I find a tidbit that makes me feel better about a loss. *Sometimes* I just like to follow the trends, because I love numbers and stats. Wins of course are the best stat, but batting average and ERA are good ones, too. I can do the math in my head and sometimes I find a mistake someone made. Yep, even in the modern age of computers smarter than a spaceship, mistakes slip through.

Sitting with the paper in my hands and the cup of coffee on my beat up wrought-iron table, I contemplate adding to the air pollution by lighting the day's second cigarette. The first one was when I was still sky-clad standing on my balcony watching that gorgeous view of this beautiful city. I have cut down on my smoking, quite a bit in fact, but cigarette number two was calling my name and my will to deny it was fading fast. Surrendering, I reach my hand out to the pack sitting aside the lizard-jaw ashtray when I finally notice this girl walking back and forth in front of my shop.

I say girl because I am an older woman and, like many older people, everyone under forty is a girl or boy to me. It's a rude thought of course; after all, I am not sure how she identifies herself and I like to respect people even if I have not spoken to them yet. These young people are fascinating to me in the way I was quaint and special to the generations before me. I know, you did not come here to listen to me talk about the modern sociopolitical issues related to identity; you came here to hear (see what I did there) about the demon. I'm getting there, but that was later in the day and this young person (the girl) has not even told me her name yet.

No, she is walking past my flower shop looking up at the big empty office building next door. No one is there now; all the offices having moved to a newer building to my right over a year ago. But this young woman was determined to find the address on the paper that she had in hand. In her other hand was her smartphone, which looked a lot smarter than mine, and I began to wonder why she was not using the phone instead of the analog crumpled white paper with scrawled writing on it. I can see the writing through the thin paper thanks to the sunlight behind the young woman-person but cannot make out the details. My eyes are not that good anymore.

She stands for a few seconds pondering the abandoned office building. I light my cigarette and inhale (glorious, oh so glorious. Don't fret; neither the cigarette nor the demon kill me.) the first smoke of cigarette number two. As I do, I take the time to check her out. The young woman is pretty, with bright eyes. Her clothes are smart, but comfortable. Her hair is professional, but there is rebellion there: this young lady is not going to let the modern capitalist grind take away her culture. I like her already even though we have not spoken, and I am more than a little intrigued by what she is looking for.

The new building is not open yet, except for the cleaning crews who come in through the parking garage. No one is in the old building, so who or what is she looking for? I admit it took me a few minutes before I realized she might be looking for me. We do not get many folks on Market Street this time of day, you see. Of course we get cars, but the foot traffic is almost nothing. Most of the people who do come by are joggers, drifters, and cops.

She walks past me again as if I was not there. I mean who cares about an old woman in front of a flower shop smoking down her second cigarette of the day? I watch as the young woman walks to the new building, shakes her head and lets her hands fall to her side in defeat.

"Can I help you?" I crush out the cigarette.

She looks my way, seeing me for the first time and her eyes light up. "Oh, I hope so! I am looking for an office on Market Street and it should be here, but I cannot find it!"

"What's the number?"

"1426-D Market."

I giggle. Like one of my favorite book characters, I am a giggler. I cannot help but giggle when something strikes me. Oh, I know I should be dignified, sure, but, man, some days I cannot help it when the giggle man comes a preaching. I just have to let him in.

I manage to keep the giggles to a minimum, though. No need to be rude. "Uhm, say what is your name? Names help us make better conversations."

She walks over and extends her hand. "Alex Jones."

"Alex, I am Dorithea. Pleased to meet you." I shake her hand once, firmly, and let it go just as my papa taught me. "And I think you are looking for me."

The smile fades. "Sorry?"

I point to the sign above my door, announcing the Rita's Market Street Flowers and among other things, the address. I see her eyes grow wide, first in astonishment and then in confusion.

"I didn't even notice." She looks back to my face. "I am looking for an expert in trends and futures."

I nod. Of course she is. This is starting to make sense. "Well, that is me. I do more than rose buds, you see." I pause to let that sink in. "Who sent you?"

"My boss, Nancy Weller."

That explains it. "Oh Nancy! I have not seen her since the Trighton deal. Well," I stand up and grab my coffee and paper, "suppose we had better go inside. It's going to be a hot day."

To be honest, I did not think Alex Jones was going to follow me inside. I passed through the rows of flowers, perennials, annuals, and vines and made my way to the counter. I opened the small refrigerator I have there, filled with sodas, water, and the odd sports drink, and pulled out something green and fizzy. I was behind the counter ringing up the null sale for myself when I spied Alex making her way in. She stops briefly to examine a lily, but finally lands in front of the counter with her hands folded in front of her.

"I really think this is some mistake. I am not Ms. Weller's assistant. I am a junior purchaser on her staff."

Poor Alex, I am thinking at this point, but I do not say out loud. "No mistake. Nancy does order flowers from my shop, but she uses my online store for that. She only sends someone around when a particular deal needs to be done." I turn the cap and listen for the slow escape of the carbonation. "Something very important."

Alex frowns, looking around my store for some indication that I can help her. "I am in negotiation with Underworlds Farming to purchase corn for a variety of customers and uses. The problem is their crop forecasts are..."

"Impossible to predict? They always steer the numbers this way or that, trying to throw off your profits. Problem is they control so much farming land and have damn cheap labor."

Alex's face is changing a bit while we talk. I can almost see her wanting to believe that I can help her. It takes most people a while to understand what I can truly do for them. Some never come around.

"Right? In fact, I am not sure what they pay their workers."

I shrug. "Next to nothing. They cornered a market a long time ago. During the war, I think. The big war here on Earth. The Allies needed grains and Underworlds was happy to cooperate. That was my first run-in with them."

"Are you talking about World War II?"

"No, before that. The Great War, at least our part in it."

Alex shakes her head and I can see I am losing her again.

"Well never mind history. What you need is some information that you can take with you into the negotiations. Do you know who is representing Underworlds?"

"A Mr. Lucien Bahall."

I cringe. "Lucien Bhal. Pronounced like a baseball or football."

"Oh, I... didn't realize."

"Well he began life, such as it is, as just Bhal. He took on Lucien a few centuries ago." I reach down under the counter and get my not-so smartphone. When I pop back up Alex's wide eyes are telling me everything I need to know.

"I need to call someone to cover the store for me. When is the meeting set for?"

Alex looks down at her phone and back up to me. I know she wants to walk right out of my store; I keep hitting her with information and it's starting to weigh her down.

"Six-thirty tonight."

"That gives us all day, then. Good, I think I can have you ready by then." I call up my friend John, a retiree who has been a lifelong flower geek. He watches the store for me from time to time. As usual he agrees to help, and I take Alex Jones aside while we wait to begin explaining this brave new world to her.

"I would not think a druid would eat meat."

Alex is watching me, picking at her fries more than eating them. It's been three hours and I needed a food break. So did she, even though Alex would never admit it. Alex Jones is a tough woman who does not quite believe in magic. Even now. But she is not going to let on because that might make her look weak.

"Where did you get that idea?"

"Most Wiccans I know are vegans or vegetarians."

I giggle but fight down most of the laughter. After all, this is a common problem I run into. "I am not a Wiccan. I am a druid. Old school. Celtic. The Old Ways. From the Anatolian tradition of Celts. I don't turn into animals, at least not very often, and I don't keep all the holidays either. I have never even read Campbell or Carpenter or Fitzgerald. Are you getting it yet?"

"No." Alex drops a fry to her plate. "No, I don't fucking get it!" Alex crosses her arms and shakes her head. "I am not saying you don't know what you are doing, but I refuse to believe you are some kind of moldy old magician!"

"We are judges, not magicians. I mean, there is magic of course. We deal with the spirits of the land, just like the people here," I point around my head, "once did. Like they still do when they can. Before the new people came, willing or unwilling, and messed things up. It's quiet now, better than it used to be. At least with the spirits, though the people are still angry."

"How is all of this supposed to help me negotiate with Lucien Bhal?"

I sit back, sipping at my soda. "You won't be, not until I have softened him up. You will have to deal with his associate, a woman named Aliza Vek. Vek is a real hard-ass with numbers, but I think you can beat her. Just remember, no matter what she tries, if you stick to the numbers you can break her. I will give you a few charms to protect you. Vek and Bhal don't play fair."

"If that is true, then why do we deal with them?"

I shrug. Great question. "Because they have something we want. Bhal and his associates are ruthless, true, but they play by a set of rules. They play hard and they play to win. They are not devils any more than I am a witch." I lean in, because I want her to really take what I am about to say to heart. "But they are bastards who will make you wish you had never set foot in the negotiation room with them. Bring your A-game and you can win. I'll cover all the spooky magic parts, keep you safe in that regard, but you have to bring the rest." I smile. "Along with the numbers I ran for you."

Alex nods and then, somewhat reluctantly, smiles. "Are you going to paint me blue?"

We both laugh. This is what I needed to see. Nancy was smart to choose Alex Jones for this; the young woman had the ability to roll with punches. Most folks would have checked out two hours ago.

"Only from the breasts down."

We arrive fifteen minutes early and stop by the top office. Nancy is there, looking frazzled. I send her off with a cup of tea to wait for the results. Aliza Vek is seated at the fake wooden table, ice-blue eyes staring at us through the glass wall. She is wearing a matching business suit that is all points. I bet the toe seams of her stockings are perfectly level, too. I nod to Vek and then send Alex in with a word of encouragement. I wait for them to shake hands and sit down before heading down the hallway. I find an office marked private, gently grab the brass handle, and let myself in.

This office is different. The curtains are drawn and only a little light is coming in. The rug and furniture are all dark colors. Drink bottles sit on one wooden cabinet and some mints and other candies sit on the one opposite. In the middle of the room, wearing a black suit, button-down shirt, and a red tie while standing over a map of Georgia, is a dark-haired man. In one hand is a drink.

I have to laugh at how cliché Lucien can be sometimes.

"Thea." His voice is smooth, the lyrical murmurings of a lover who knows how well he made you climax.

"Lucien." I find a chair and sit down, grabbing an ashtray and pulling out my smokes. My fingers tingle when they touch the ashtray, so I know it has some spirit on it. It could just be a minor djinn tasked with listening and recording everything we say. It could be an old lover forced into the glass ashtray to distract me. I make sure I light up one of my special cigarettes and tap the ashes into the glass.

Lucien looks over at me, notices my cigarette, and then looks down to the ashtray. "That wasn't very nice."

I smile. "I seem to remember the last time we were in a room like this, you made a point of saying that playing nice was for losers."

"The '80s were a different time, old friend." He smoothly settles into the seat in front of me. Lucien taps his glass with his index finger and the amber liquid refills. "We were bar-barians back then."

I cross my legs and check the laces on my five-dollar sneakers. "I was talking about last year."

"Well, times have changed. We don't really like the current social climate. Too contentious all around."

"Current president seems like he'd be your type."

Now it is Lucien's turn to laugh. "Do you know what he did to that football league he bought into? No," Lucien takes a sip of his drink, "we don't want him in our business. You mortals can keep him."

"Now that is not nice."

Lucien tilts his head to one side. "Sorry. In any case our client is eager to sell this corn and we need a good price."

Of course they do. I had a sneaking suspicion there was more to this deal than a good price on the next couple harvests.

"What for? Surely you have enough money to buy whatever it is you want."

"What we need is something money cannot buy." Lucien flicks his fingers and an image of an idol appears. I recognize it of course, any magician worth their charms would recognize it.

Squat, with the head of a vulture and the body of a bear, this creature sits in its pose, seemingly nothing more than stone. A mortal would never recognize the subtle bits of life evident in the large eyes.

"I'm sorry, what are we talking about here?"

"We want to buy our brother back. The mortal who owns his form won't part with it for less than $100 million. Our firm would balk at such a price, so we have to find a way to negotiate that down."

I sit very still, taking an inventory of the office. It lies just outside the mortal realms, though you would not know it just by looking. There are two or three other items just like the ashtray, with spirits in them. Here, right next door to the other realms, the spirits have more power than normal.

"Your brother was imprisoned by mortals. For good reason."

Lucien waves his drink hand. "I am not here to judge events from two thousand years ago. It is time for Bhal to come home."

All demons are called Bhal, you see. The differences in their names are subtle and beyond what mortals can perceive. I can hear the subtle differences, but only after a century of practice.

"So how can I help get this done? There was no accident you maneuvered Nancy into sending her broker to me. Let's not beat around the bush, Lucien."

He smiles, that charming and smooth smile that puts a curl in your toes. "Now we are getting somewhere." Lucien stands and walks over to the map of Georgia, dragging it in front of me. He sets his drink down next to a small town south of Atlanta, about thirty miles down I-75.

"The mortal is a baseball fan."

Yep, I had a feeling we were going there. Lucien sits on the table, a lot closer than I am comfortable with. This is all part of his crowding strategy to get inside someone's head. I shift my legs around and light another cigarette. The smoke drifts between the two of us, keeping his energy at bay.

"And an old lady in Hartown owns two balls and two cards. She has left them to a certain druid in Atlanta. If perhaps she could be convinced to sell them to our client instead..."

"Those are rare items I was going to add to the city's spirit." I take a drag of the cigarette and let out some smoke in Lucien's face. "Why would I want to let," and I almost slip and say her name, "that old lady sell them to your mortal?" Lucien's spirits were there to collect the old woman's name and I almost let them have her! Thankfully, I managed to keep the name from my lips and my thoughts. Son of a bitch is crafty.

"The mortal wants them, but the old lady has promised them to you. Now, we don't want this to get ugly, but if we can convince the old woman to sell, we can have Bhal for $50 million."

"And Nancy gets the price she is asking?"

"Actually about twenty cents lower. That's how much we want Bhal back. Everyone is happy if this goes through."

"Except me. What do I get?"

Lucien sits down. "What do you want?"

I am a little pissed that Lucien is trying to rope me into this. He and his firm know I try and protect the people and the city, even the rich folks who never buy a single house fern from me. This is my city and I take that sacred duty as seriously as my ancestors in Galicia used to. I light a third cigarette and slow down time a little. Since the room touches the mortal realms, I can put my knowledge to good use. Lucien might not even notice me conjuring this close. And if he did, there was little he could do to stop me.

I try and think this through, taking each thread and weaving it into the big picture. The firm wants enough money from the corn sales to justify paying for the return of Bhal. A mortal client wants a large sum for the idol but will part with it for less if they can have an old woman's baseball memorabilia. I want those items myself, to strengthen the city. I have an idea, but I need a few more answers.

"How long does he have left in his prison?" I ease the time back to normal so Lucien can answer.

"One thousand and thirty-two years."

Bingo. "So he won't mind spending another few years with me."

Lucien puts his drink down.

"How long will the mortal live? Without interference from you, of course."

"We evaluated her life choices and predict thirty to forty years."

"All right. Here is what I can offer you." I match his posture, crushing my cigarette out on the ashtray. I can feel the spirit squirming. Good.

"I am listening." Lucien picks up his drink, ready to say no the moment I ask for too much.

"I hold on to Bhal until the woman dies. You get him back when those items come to me. I convince the old lady to part with her items, for a good sum. Nancy gets her price and twenty-five cents lower. I ran the numbers, you and your clients still come out way ahead."

Lucien holds the drink to his lips for a three count, thinking about my offer and doing the math inside of his head. His firm will still come out far ahead.

"All right. I think we can agree to that in principle. Shall we join Ms. Jones and Ms. Vek?"

By the time we get back to them, Alex and Aliza are shaking hands and smiling. Aliza never smiles unless someone gives her a good game; she can't stand shitty negotiators.

"Well, how did it go?" Lucien is pleased with himself. Of course, he has no idea what I will be doing with Bhal while the little bastard is in my possession, but Lucien is a sadist even when his own kind are concerned. I am sure he would approve.

Aliza nods to Alex. "When Ms. Jones's contract is up we should make her an offer."

"I was thinking the same thing." Alex shoots back and we all have a good laugh. Poor Aliza is a lifer in ways Alex does not understand yet.

"Well then, shall we collect Nancy and grab some dinner?"

"Better idea. How about a Braves' game? Lucien is buying!"

Lucien smiles. "I love baseball!"

Aliza is less enthused. "I might need to change."

It's almost two in the morning as Alex and I sit in my flower shop, all grins. The bullpen had pitched a perfect three innings to win the game.

"So how long have you been a fan of baseball?"

"Longer than I have been a fan of magic." I am stirring my coffee, letting the waves of liquid churn around the cup's edge. "We had to watch through the fence, but my daddy made sure we were fans."

Alex nods. I think she is on the verge of collapsing, after all the ups and downs of the last day, but to her credit she is holding it together. "Say, is this how it always is? I mean, being a druid?"

"In the old days we were go-betweens for the tribes. We protected the sacred places and sometimes, we desecrated those of our enemies." I look up. "I won't lie, our history has as much bad as it does good. As much blood on our hands. Just like anyone." I set the spoon I am using down. "But I think we did okay today. Things might have gotten nasty if we hadn't brokered that deal."

"You did all the work."

I shake my head. "No, I didn't! What I did was let myself get backed into a corner. At least I have thirty or forty years to figure out how to keep Bhal in his prison." I stand up, no longer interested in my coffee. "But the city and Nancy's reputation are intact for now."

"Can I ask you a question?" Alex stands up, her expression thoughtful.

"Of course."

"What does it take to do," she looks up at the ceiling and then back to me, "all of this?"

I smile. There is something special about Alex Jones; I guess I sensed it from the moment I saw her on the sidewalk. Yes, she could be a magician, if not in my tradition then in some tradition.

"I open up for business at nine. Come by and find out."

SKIN DEEP

L. N. Hunter

"How original," drawled the tall, black-suited man standing within the pentagram. "You humans! Is eternal life *really* the best you can come up with?" He sucked deeply on his cigarette and casually blew several smoke rings: first, a perfect triangle, then a square, a pentagon, and finally, a hexagon. He flicked the spent cigarette away and ground it out, his shiny black wingtips making scratches on the elaborate parquet floor.

"I want to remain young and healthy, too—I'm not going to suffer Tithonus's fate, when he forgot to ask to stop aging." The young woman knew she looked good. Her inheritance had already paid for a few little nips and tucks, but her youthful beauty wouldn't last forever unless she made sure to include that in the bargain. She thought for a moment. "And no tricks about having to find special food or drink. No killing things to absorb their life essence or whatever. I'm a vegan, you know."

The man lifted another cigarette to his lips, where it spontaneously ignited. "You ask a lot, my dear Emilia Beatrice Kilburn." He smiled and exhaled a thick cloud of smoke, which grew and swirled around his body. When it dissipated, a red-skinned demon stood in his place, horns grazing the ceiling of the private library. He had the same orange eyes as the man, and the same cigarette dangling from his thin lips. "Is there anything else?" Smoke drifted from the demon's mouth as he spoke. "Or is that an acceptable exchange for your soul?"

Emilia knew that dealing with demonkind was fraught with danger, but she was clever and had done her homework. "One more thing. I don't want an injury or illness to leave me in any way disabled. I don't want to suffer *any* accidents."

The demon removed the cigarette from his mouth and smiled widely, showing all his yellowed teeth. "Smart girl, indeed. Your Daddy-funded education is paying off, isn't it?" He gestured at the elegant oil paintings lining the walls and shelves of antique books. "Would you like *more* riches to go with your very long life? A country to rule, perhaps? You could be a—what do you mortals call it—a 'media personality' with hordes of adoring fans." He looked around the room. "I can see that you're used to comfort, and you didn't think twice about ruining this beautiful floor with your pentagram. Surely you could do with *some* help to keep you, as they say, in the style to which you are accustomed..."

Emilia didn't hesitate. She shook her head. "Nope, no way. I'm rich enough already, and sensible investing will keep me going. I'm smart enough to look after my own finances, thank you very much. The more I ask *you* for, on the other hand, the more chance there is of you finding some loophole."

The demon heaved an exaggerated sigh. "Some people. All I'm trying to do is make your life much more pleasurable."

"For you, you mean, not me! I'm not falling for your lies."

The dark prince pouted. "I could take offense at that. I never utter falsehoods. Your... research... must have told you that. You know, I've always thought the title 'Prince of Lies' incredibly unfair." He shrugged. "We just don't always tell the complete truth."

Emilia scowled and she shouted, "Tempt me not, foul fiend!" When the demon's face froze and his stare lanced into her, she felt her heart pause. Had she taken a step too far?

Then he roared with laughter. "The old lines really are the best."

"Eternal life, that's what I want," she muttered. "No physical or mental degradation, no accidents. And that's it."

"Perhaps I might be permitted to make one more suggestion?"

Emelia eyed him suspiciously but let him proceed.

"Existence as an unchanging immortal can be a nuisance; I speak from experience. Your friends will wonder why you don't appear to age and, should you do something to attract unwanted attention, it could be difficult to escape the eye of the oh-so-critical public." He pursed his lips. "I could give you deliberate conscious control of your appearance." He paused and let the edges of his mouth twitch upward. "That is, if you think it could be helpful."

Emilia stiffened and licked her lips. This was something she hadn't considered. Her face went blank as she thought about the possibilities. If she always looked the same, she'd have to keep moving every few years, and ensuring continuous access to her wealth would require a lot of effort. On the other hand, she could allow herself to gradually take on the appearance of age and, simultaneously, introduce a younger cousin or distant niece to the household. This young relative would inherit everything from her doting elder, and Emilia could perpetuate herself that way. There'd be few awkward questions. She couldn't think of any disadvantage of being able to alter her appearance but, remembering that the demon said he never lied, she asked, "What am I missing here?"

"Why, nothing at all! You think it, you look it—what could be simpler, my dear Ms. Kilburn?" The demon inhaled on his cigarette, causing the end to glow as brightly as his orange eyes, then shrugged again. As if he'd been reading her mind, he said, "If you'd rather not invent nieces and prefer to spend eternity running from people, that's entirely up to you. I only make the offer; you make the decision."

Emilia stared into his unblinking eyes until hers started to water and she had to look away. "Okay then, I agree."

The demon's form snapped back to the tall, lawyerly appearance, and he dropped his second cigarette on to the mahogany floor, once again grinding it into the varnish. He extracted a parchment and an ornate quill from inside his suit. Stepping forward, he crossed the lines of the pentagram with ease and pricked Emilia's forearm with the quill, drawing blood.

"Ow!" She flinched. Then she paused, rubbing her arm where she'd been stabbed, and asked in a weak voice, "Wait, you could've left the pentagram any time?"

"Of course, my dear. Your petty patterns mean nothing to me. I came because your soul called to me, not because of your spells and scribbles." He held the parchment out to her. "Please do verify that this corresponds with your desires." He offered the quill, charged with Emilia's blood, and said in a deeper voice that reverberated as if they were standing in a room considerably larger than the library, "and then please sign."

Emelia read the brief document from beginning to end three times, carefully considering every nuance of language, looking for tricks and hidden escape clauses. She finally concluded that the contract was accurate and correct, and signed. The parchment seemed to suck the ink—her blood—from the quill. The ink was dry by the time she handed the parchment and now-drained quill back to the demon. She started to speak but faltered, with a suddenly dry mouth. She swallowed and tried again, managing no more than a hoarse whisper. "I do have one question."

The tall man raised an eyebrow.

"If I'm immortal, how will you get my soul?"

The man's lips turned up at the edges, the smile not reaching his hypnotic eyes. "My dear Ms. Kilburn, your soul is not the important thing here and it never was; the promise is enough. What do you think I would do with a soul? It's an insubstantial, trivial thing and not a part of the physical universe; I can affect it as much as a flea can inconvenience an elephant. No, it's your torment I enjoy, and *that* doesn't have to wait until your death."

He started to chuckle as he faded from existence. Emilia was left with the echo of his laugh and the thick smell of cigarette smoke, along with a sick feeling in her stomach.

She expected to feel different, but nothing seemed to change in the weeks that followed. She caught herself wondering if she'd really summoned a demon and exchanged her soul for eternal life, or if she was suffering from some mental illness. How could she tell? She swallowed an uncomfortable giggle at the thought that all she had to do was wait for a very long time and see whether she died or not.

Assuming she had made a deal with a demon, Emilia considered all the things she could do now: travel the world, learn to play a musical instrument—heck, several. Then she realized that normal people—*mortal* people—could do, and did do, these things; all that was different was she had more time in which to do them.

So, she did the same as most people, rich or poor. She procrastinated.

And while she procrastinated, she thought about her sister, the initial trigger for her deal-making. Suzanne had died after a battle with leukemia, despite the application of the best medical attention vast sums of inherited money could buy. Emilia wanted to save her sister, or to at least extend her unfairly shortened life. Once conventional medicine had conceded defeat, she followed many paths on the internet and elsewhere in search of treatments. At best, some of the legion of self-proclaimed healers alleviated Suzanne's pain a little, but most were charlatans, mere snake-oil sellers.

A week before Suzanne died, Emilia came across a website that looked different from the others. Nothing more than an old-fashioned form, white text boxes on a plain black background, inviting visitors to describe what would drive them to make the ultimate sacrifice. Normally, Emilia would have closed the browser window and moved on, but she was desperate—Suzanne had endured a particularly bad episode that day—so she filled in the form. She said she loved her sister and couldn't imagine living without her. She paused briefly and added, "Please allow her a few more years? Just a few. That's all I ask."

As soon as she hit Enter, the page cleared, and a line of text appeared: *Your plea has been received; if we deem you worthy, you will receive instructions.*

Emilia sighed and turned off her laptop. What had she expected anyway?

A week passed. Suzanne died.

Emilia forgot about the website but, several weeks after her sister's funeral, a small, neatly wrapped black parcel arrived in the mail. As she extracted a slim book, a note slid out of the package. She picked it up and read: *You, not your sister, have been deemed worthy; follow these instructions.*

In disgust, Emilia threw the book in the back of a drawer and ignored it.

Several months passed before she stumbled across it again. She took it out for a closer look and idly examined the cover. *How ridiculous,* she thought, *a book on demonology.* But, as she read, she started to wonder if it would work. She tracked down other sources on the internet, some directing her to obscure libraries, hidden bookstores, and shadowy museums.

Though she couldn't bring her sister back, she could at least make sure she didn't suffer a similar pathetic, painful end herself.

And now, immortality beckoned, if she believed the demon... If she believed her mind.

As the years passed, Emilia attracted more and more comments from friends about her youthful appearance. She laughed and said, "You can't believe how much I spent at Gerardo's and the spa. It takes a lot of time and effort to look this good." To her closest friends, she confessed to hiding a lot under make-up, and admitted that the best cosmetic surgery could offer was paying off. However, she realized it was time to think about changing her appearance.

She stared at herself in the mirror and wondered what to do. After a moment, feeling somewhat self-conscious, she commanded, "Get older."

Nothing happened.

She remembered what the demon had offered: control of her appearance. But what did that really mean? She suddenly grasped that she had to worry about the details, every single wrinkle and blemish. She couldn't be vague. *Shit!*

She also realized that she couldn't picture what her face should look like at her correct age, quite a few years older than she currently appeared. The only thing that came to mind was a vague impression of the crow's feet around her friend's eyes, not having ever closely examined the precise pattern of creases—who really ever looks at a friend's face in critical detail? She opened her laptop and searched for pictures of women her age. It was harder than she expected, since most people tended to try to hide signs of aging in anything they allow to be made public. In the age range from about 25 to 45, people in the public eye pay ever-increasing attention to retaining their youth before relenting and accepting the effects of time. Eventually, Emilia had a number of photographs of the same people at different ages, so she could study how age affected their appearance.

She placed the laptop beside her mirror and, switching her gaze between her reflection and the screen, concentrated on precisely copying the patterns of small wrinkles from the pictures to the skin around her eyes and lips, *willing* the creases into place. Eventually, exhausted and with a throbbing headache, she achieved satisfactory results; there was a stranger in the mirror, but a stranger who moved like her and wore expressions she was accustomed to seeing in her reflection. She even managed an amused thought as she went to bed: first thing in the morning, she'd be applying make-up to hide most of this painstaking work.

Something felt wrong when she woke up. Her mouth was numb, and her left eye wouldn't open properly. There was a sticky, pulling sensation as she lifted her head from the pillow. She staggered to the bathroom and switched on the light. She stared uncomprehendingly at the mirror, then screamed.

Her face had melted, at least that's what it looked like. It was as if gravity had caused everything to sag while she slept. The skin was tight on the right side, while loose, flabby folds had collected on the left, covering her eye and making her mouth droop and drool.

"No-no-no-no!" she slurred. "This can't be happening." She dropped to the floor and fought back tears as she tried to figure out what was going on. It couldn't be an illness; the demon had promised that.

She replayed what exactly he'd said: deliberate conscious control. Then she understood.

She had conscious control of her looks, but no one had said anything about *unconscious* effects. *The bastard! The bloody bastard! No wonder he'd been laughing.* Was this going to happen every night? More importantly for the moment, could she fix it?

She quickly pushed and pulled and *thought* her skin back to a face shape, but she could see it still wasn't her own face. Something looked not quite right, but she couldn't tell what—some almost imperceptible detail was wrong, throwing the whole out of shape. As with most of her friends, her phone was full of selfies, so she had plenty of material showing what she looked like. She pored over the photos; move this freckle here, sharpen that line there, compare the results with her photographs, and move on to the next patch of skin. An hour later, she recognized herself. Then she set about aging herself again.

She got to work very late that day, carrying with her the worry that the backs of her ears might not be quite right, along with other areas she didn't have any photos of or couldn't see in her mirrors. She couldn't tell if people were staring at her, or if it was merely her frantic imagination.

The following morning, and every morning after, she discovered the answer to her first question: yes, this was going to happen every night.

She gave up her job; it wasn't as if she needed the money. Instead, she spent most of her days working on her face.

Emilia stopped going out in the evening after that incident with Steve. Or was it Stefan..., or Scott? She couldn't remember; she never paid much attention to their names. A cute surfer blond with a hot body, whom she'd picked up in her favorite nightclub while wearing the face and body of her younger self.

Fueled by tequila, they lurched from the taxi and made their way through Emilia's house. They passed the door to the library, a room Emilia hadn't entered since her demonic visit, and staggered up the stairs, giggling and discarding clothes along the way.

At first, Steve—or whoever he was—took control, and Emilia let the tingle of pleasure run up and down her body. After a while, growing impatient, she pushed him back on to the bed and stroked and fondled and sucked and pinched until the world had shrunk to just the pair of them. It didn't take long before she was on the brink of orgasm.

"Yes, yes, yes, yes," Emilia panted, eyes closed and hips moving in time with the thrusting beneath her.

Steve slowed, then halted completely.

Eyes still closed, Emilia licked her lips and murmured, "Don't stop." When nothing happened, she opened her eyes to see a shocked expression below her.

"Your body...? What's happening to it?"

Shit! She could feel her face sagging and looked down to see her breasts stretching across the bed, drooping over the sides. "Wait, it's nothing. Wait!"

She pulled her breasts into a bundle in her arms and concentrated on bringing her body back to normal, but the mood was shattered.

Steve pushed her away and scrabbled out from underneath, thudding onto the floor. Mouth flapping soundlessly, he stared at her for a moment longer, then ran for the door, not even taking time to collect his clothes.

In any case, she thought afterwards, when she stopped crying, *it'll be easier if I go to bed earlier; I'll have more time the next day to fix my face.* She started crying again at the idea.

Another year passed, with Emilia getting better at pulling her face and body back into shape. She spent fewer and fewer hours on the task each day, but daydreaming could be disastrous.

Maybe it was time to finally start her journey round the world, though out of necessity rather than desire. Now, she'd be sticking to places where few people would see her.

Over the next few decades, Emilia contributed to cryptozoological legends about strange semi-humans sighted in various parts of the world. She was adept at snapping back to a normal person now—she had a repertoire of appearances—but she found it impossible to make her mask persist when her thoughts strayed. She became accustomed to being a wrinkled, sagging creature.

In her eighth decade, she caught herself wondering why she had asked the demon for eternal life. She'd only thought of avoiding pain and death, but could those be much worse than her current lonely life? Emilia smiled wryly at the thought of rejecting his offer of riches and comfort because she thought she knew better. What did all the money from her investments mean now?

Sometime during her second century, she spent several months unsuccessfully trying to kill herself. Wounds closed up within minutes; poisons sweated themselves out of her body; drowning just left her feeling very thirsty.

She entombed herself via a cave explosion and existed for thirteen years as a blob of human porridge squeezed beneath heavy rocks, until she finally got bored and oozed free. She had only the dimmest recollection of that time. She might have gone insane for some of that period. Or maybe a human brain doesn't work properly when it's spread pancake-thin.

Regaining at least the semblance of a human form after that, she travelled from country to country, from continent to continent, looking for a solution to her problem. She ventured to monasteries high in the Himalayas, grateful for the warmth of the shaggy coat of fur she grew. She visited hermitages deep in arid deserts, where she found her dwindling wealth could still open doors. She conferred with occultists and sorcerers, witches and warlocks, in the hope that they could fix her physical form. Despite most being as ineffectual as the medical snake-oil peddlers from so long ago, Emilia gained knowledge from those who were true. She came to understand many mystical secrets and esoteric magics, but there was no cure for her condition.

Perhaps, then, she could find a spell to call the demon back to her, to plead for a renegotiation of the deal, a trade of some of her life for her appearance, but the closest she got was hearing the whisper of his laugh on the wind. She learned that the only currency demons were interested in was souls, and she'd already promised the solitary one she owned.

She trained herself to tune and modulate her senses. With her ability to change her shape, Emilia could grow ears which could hear better than a bat's, and eyes which could see further than an eagle's. She found she could travel without being seen, making herself a pale, insubstantial cloud which could pass through any gap. She could even detach small fragments of her body and morph them into other objects. But she still had to concentrate on maintaining a human appearance most of the time she was awake, and she had to rebuild her body after every period of sleep.

She could be a comic book superhero, if she cared, but Emilia Beatrice Kilburn no longer considered herself a part of humanity. She even resented those dumb humans who had never suffered as she did.

Emilia eventually returned to her home city, which seemed to have changed very little in the centuries since she was last there. Wandering the streets like some homeless bag-lady, she stumbled across a library which still had retro computer terminals. She was surprised that such a place still existed—probably the result of a bequest from some wealthy, old-fashioned reader. She entered and, conscious of stares from the librarian and the handful of other occupants of the building, sat down at one of the terminals.

She typed in the address of the website which had started all this, intending to ask for help again. Hoping for more than a "site not found" message, she expected to see an empty form to type in but, instead, the screen displayed an already filled-in request. There was a name, Ernest Roberts, and a street address on the page. A map site gave her directions to a gated community in the suburbs.

She made her way to the man's house, passing by the community's security guards with ease. It was a large, blocky building with tall casement windows and a solid oak front door, and reminded her of the house in which she'd first met her demon. Did she still own that house, she wondered. Her memory didn't seem to be as good as it used to be; the demon had promised mental health, but it seemed that didn't include memory. One of the windows on the first floor showed some light, so she peered in. She stumbled back at what she saw, but then laughed and immediately knew what she had to do next. Maybe she could gain another soul, another chance.

She eased her form through a gap in the window frame and appeared in a cloud of smoke within the pentagram chalked on the floor.

The man stared at the tall black-dressed woman in surprise.

Emilia materialized a lit cigarette and popped it between her lips. She inhaled deeply, paused for a few seconds, then let the smoke escape in a long slow breath. She took the cigarette from her mouth and studied the glowing tip for a few seconds, before looking at the man.

"What do you most desire, my dear Ernest Oliver Roberts?"

She let her eyes glow orange, as she smiled, showing all her teeth.

THE WORKING
OF WAX

Jen Sexton-Riley

The number went to voicemail. Again.

Liza ended the call without leaving another message. She took a deep, uneven breath, let it out with closed eyes and tossed the phone onto the worn futon that took up half the floor space of her tiny studio apartment. It bounced off the lumpy surface, skittered across the clay-dust-covered floor and came to rest among the clean spaces left vacant three weeks ago by the removal of every single one of Liza's sculptures.

"I have to have your work," Aims had said, talking through a mouthful of sashimi.

Aimsley Sharp, owner and curator of The Sharp Gallery in Pioneer Square, had finally spotted her sculptures laid out on a blanket during the Third Thursday art walk, where Liza was trying to catch his discerning eye. Or at least earn some grocery money. With a gasp, he'd removed his pale vicuña jacket and, glancing up and down the street, draped it over her work, shielding his discovery from the competition's prying eyes. This was it. The fairytale moment was here. Liza had dreamed of it every Third Thursday, summer after summer, as she staked out her spot on the sidewalk, kicking away the cigarette butts, smoothing her blanket and arranging her sculptures as close as she could to the vast, glittering windows of The Sharp.

Liza's vision swam in the warm summer air. It was actually happening.

Gesturing to three men in silver Sharp Gallery coveralls who seemed to appear from nowhere, Aimsley Sharp placed his large hands on Liza's shoulders and steered her through the unmarked side door of a sleek minimalist space that only hinted at being a restaurant. He sat her at a lone table in the back. Craning her neck toward the windows, Liza saw the silver-clad men scooping up her sculptures and walking toward The Sharp. Liza couldn't find her voice, which was just as well. Aimsley Sharp had a lot to say.

"All of it. And I need it now. Don't worry, they're in good hands. The best. My Sharp men know their jobs, or they don't have them," Aimsley said, summoning a waiter with a snap.

Liza felt out of place in the rarefied interior. She patted down her wild shock of hair and took a deep breath of cold, conditioned air, the silvery atmosphere of planet Sharp, scented with amber and vetiver. She felt as if she hadn't inhaled in a very long time.

"Now look," he continued, jabbing a manicured index finger at the swirling, violet glow of the table's surface. "La Biennale di Venezia, as you must know, only happens every two years. There's only one spot left in our pavilion's allotted exhibition space. Now. Normally I wouldn't take a risk like this. But work like this? From a—forgive me, but from a nobody in the street such as yourself? I need it. I need it all, I need it now, and I am going to make a splash in Venice like they've never seen. I mean we. We are. Give me your address. Oh, and your name. Sashimi? What's your favorite? Bluefin tuna belly? Yellow fin? Squid? Urchin? How about some of each. Excuse me, sir! Champagne! Or plum wine perhaps... say, you are old enough to drink, aren't you? Oh, never mind. Who cares!"

Aimsley appeared to like that Liza was overwhelmed into acquiescence by his expensive food and his uniformed minions. It seemed to delight him to discover, on inquiring about her background, that Liza had aged out of the foster care system without being adopted into a family. No surprised compassion softened his features as it usually did when Liza revealed her history to strangers. Quite the opposite. Aimsley stifled a giggle. He loved that she had nobody. No hometown, not even a mom and dad to weep proud tears over their little ragamuffin's Cinderella story. Liza was nobody, and Liza had nothing.

Aimsley Sharp's face lit up when he learned that Liza's entire world was made up of her tiny, dim apartment and her sculptures. He clearly enjoyed the widening of her eyes when he offered her the one vacant studio space left in The Sharp—third floor, all right? You prefer the fourth? I can move somebody else if you like a view?—and he chuckled when she nearly dropped his ring-polished stainless steel business card with SHARP embossed into the surface, rising five letters strong from cold, concentric circles. There was no question that Aims liked Liza accompanying him to his lakefront home with little coaxing. She wandered through its many pale rooms the next morning wearing nothing but his bespoke silver jacquard pajama top, which hung to her knees like a dress. His little urchin. His shiny new star.

Aimsley Sharp shared his Hunts Point estate only with a minimal staff. His domestic life consisted of occasional visits from a divorced sister and her young daughter. Any need he had for familial warmth was more than covered by semi-annual visits from the girl, whose photos at various ages adorned the less commanding wall spaces not dominated by enormous fields of color and writhing masses of metal, wood, ceramic, and glass.

Promises of luggage and a new wardrobe for Venice were made. Aimsley —no, please, call me Aims—encouraged Liza to accept a thick fold of crisp bills to treat herself. There would be more. Much, much more. Liza hid it in a tin on top of her nearly empty refrigerator behind the yellowing row of five birthday cards from her court-appointed special advocate, one each year since her 18th birthday.

Now, three weeks later, no luggage. No Venice wardrobe. No more where that came from. No studio. No sculptures. And no explanation. Her calls to Aims went to voicemail, one after another. Liza started to feel like she'd been had.

She tore open her last package of ramen noodles and eyed the dry block. She broke it in half, put one piece back in the package for tomorrow, and tossed the other to Knot, who sat dangling its legs over the edge of the kitchen table. Knot caught the dry noodles just barely, and stood hugging the block to its chest with both its golden beeswax arms.

"Put that in some water and heat it up for me, will you,

Knot?"

Knot nodded, its namesake knot of twine bobbing like a ponytail from its spot embedded in the top of the beeswax poppet's head. As Knot got to work, heaving the noodle block over the pot's side, which stood as tall as the poppet's shoulders, Liza retrieved her phone from its place on the floor.

The number went to voicemail. Again.

* * *

The Sharp Gallery, a 150,000 square foot building which housed a glove factory back when everyone wore gloves no matter the weather, dominated the skyline at the edge of Seattle's industrial district. Aimsley Sharp had reimagined and renovated the cavernous historic space to house some forty-five artists in live-work studios distributed throughout the building's five floors. On the top and ground floors, seemingly endless exhibition spaces stretched nearly the length of the city block, making possible an art community almost entirely independent of the surrounding area. The Sharp's artists needed to venture out only for food and art supplies.

Liza parked her scooter, clutched her empty satchel and hurried down the sidewalk past The Sharp. Her pocket was stuffed with the money from the tin atop her refrigerator. When traffic allowed, she ducked between two parked cars and sprinted across the street, casting a quick glance up at the immense building. The Sharp stared back, its windows expressionless. The building dwarfed Althea's Arts on the other side of South Atlantic Street. The store's small, hexagonal windows glowed with golden light in The Sharp's constant shadow. Liza shouldered the door open to the sound of tinkling bells.

"Miss Liza!" cried Althea. "What a pleasure. I haven't seen you in a while. Any word yet from our wealthy cad across the street? Hey, how's Knot holding up?"

"No word yet, and I'm not holding my breath," Liza said, picking up a basket and heading into the welcoming labyrinth of paint tubes, pastels, brushes, and tools. "Knot's doing fine. You were right. It's been good for me to have some company around during all of this. You know—I was feeling really angry, like I was going to lose it and do something crazy. But then I decided I'd just take the money Sharp gave me, come down here and buy some art supplies. New clay, armature wire. I'll put all this emotion into some new sculptures. He can't take that away from me. Right?"

"That's right," Althea said. "We all know you have a temper. That's not your fault. Your life hasn't been easy. You need to use the anger, that's all. Don't let it use you. We've all heard stories about that Mr. Sharp. He collects foxy little artists as often as he collects art, you know? And—oh no."

Althea raised her eyebrows and pointed across the street. Liza walked to the window. Aimsley Sharp emerged from the stately doors of The Sharp, a young woman curled under his arm. The woman wore paint-splattered overalls and beat-up combat boots. Her plume of hair was piled high and tied with a brightly colored scarf, which floated about her head in a current of air as a car rushed past.

"Well, look at that," Althea said. "He certainly has a type," she added, gesturing toward Liza's own mop of wild hair. Liza felt her cheeks begin to burn.

The young woman's face was flushed and smiling. She and Aimsley walked past the darkened windows of the sushi place and toward the adjacent glass-walled brunch joint, The

Egg. Halfway there, he stopped and rummaged in the pocket of his pale vicuña jacket. As his companion paused and looked back, he held up something small and shiny.

"The key. The studio key. My studio key," Liza said, her voice low and measured.

"Liza?"

"He's giving her my studio key. He promised me the last studio space in The Sharp. Me! I finally had something, and now he's giving it to someone else? He takes away all of my work, won't return my calls and now he gives away my studio? This is it. Forget all this armature wire and clay and crap. I want the beeswax again, Althea. Give me the beeswax," Liza said, dropping the basket with a crash.

"Easy, Liza. Calm down, now," said Althea, her voice gentle. "We've got some really nice, pure beeswax that just came in. It's 100 percent raw, natural, and we've got it in one-ounce blocks, or..."

"No, Althea. Don't play with me. I don't want just any beeswax. I want your beeswax. That beeswax. From your bees. You know what I mean," said Liza.

"Oh come on, Liza. No. Not again. Please think this through. You're just angry right now."

"Damn right I am, and you have to give it to me if I ask," said Liza. "That's the rule. Use my anger? I'm going to use it, all right."

* * *

Step one. Take as much beeswax as you can carry by yourself and melt it down on low heat.

Liza balanced the galvanized washtub atop her hot plate as close as she could to the tiny apartment's single window. As the golden globs of raw wax began to shine and soften in the heat, Knot pushed them around in the pot with a long wooden spoon from its perch on a stack of books. The warm kitchen air became heady with sweetness.

"Don't get too close to that flame, now, Knot," Liza warned. "I need your help to get this big guy ready for action. He's got a job to do tonight. I don't want to be wasting time fixing your melty butt." Knott planted its fists on its hips and threw Liza a look of indignation. She laughed.

Liza dug through her dirty laundry pile until she found the silver jacquard pajama top she'd worn home from Aimsley Sharp's Hunts Point home. It seemed a shame to ruin such lovely fabric, she thought, as she began tearing it into strips. When the phone rang, she found herself hoping it would be Aims, that it was all a misunderstanding, and that the only loser in this mess would be the orphaned pajama bottoms, doomed to toplessness somewhere deep inside the many pale rooms in the mansion on Lake Washington.

"Liza?"

Liza's fragile hope splintered and fell to dust.

"Hey, Althea."

"Please tell me you haven't done it yet," Althea said, her musical voice taut. A soft buzzing sound softened her words.

"I'm just getting started. Knot's got your beautiful wax melting in the tub," said Liza.

"Thank goodness," Althea said. "Liza. Please. You must reconsider. Don't you remember Ivy Cook?"

Ivy Cook. That was a name Liza hadn't heard in a while. Ivy had once been another of Althea's customers, but had become the star of the ultimate cautionary tale for hot-headed sculptors. She'd postponed a coveted position with the university to travel the Floating Islands with her painting professor for an entire summer, an opportunity she simply couldn't pass up. She'd been assured the offer would remain secure until her return in September, so she packed her bags and departed on her adventure without a worry. After three weeks of close quarters on shipboard, however, Ivy and her professor had a falling out. She barely endured the rest of the trip, focusing as closely as she could on detailed renderings of native aquatic turtles and flightless birds while maintaining as little engagement with the professor as possible on a forty-seven-foot ketch with cramped sleeping quarters. On her return, Ivy was informed that her position had been given to another student. She suspected that her professor had arranged for her dismissal upon his return from the disappointing voyage. She was enraged.

"Ivy Cook came to me and demanded the wax from my bees, just like you," Althea said. "And I had to give it to her. Can you imagine how I felt after what happened?"

"Look, Althea. I'm not Ivy Cook. She must have put too much of herself into it. She must have had a paper cut, a hangnail, something. Plus she should have tethered the poppet somehow until she was sure it had the correct target and was obeying properly. I know what I'm doing. Just look at how great Knot is." Knot, hearing its name, looked up from its stirring and waved at Liza.

"It tore Ivy Cook to tiny pieces, Liza."

"I remember."

"Please. Liza. Do one thing for me."

"Anything for you, as long as you don't try to stop me."

"Just give it one night. Sleep on it. For me."

Liza tossed the phone onto the futon and sighed. She turned off the hot plate, closed the window and picked up the silver pajama top, now half torn into long strips. You wouldn't think an animated figure made of beeswax with a fabric skeleton would be strong enough to overpower someone in the prime of life, much less tear a body to tiny bits, yet this was exactly what happened to Ivy Cook. Her neighbors didn't hear a thing. It happened fast and it happened in complete silence. The scene was so bad that her apartment building was condemned and demolished, and nothing grew in the empty lot where it stood. Children held their breath and ran past only when they had to. On quiet nights passersby could hear the sound of bees there, even in winter.

Poor Ivy Cook. She deserved compassion.

Liza brought the torn silver fabric to her nostrils and inhaled. The warm scent of her own body conjured the pale rooms, the early morning light reflected from the lake's surface playing on the luminous interiors of the Sharp house, Aimsley Sharp sizing her up, his latest acquisition, through eyes like dull coins.

She looked at the empty spaces on the floor where her sculptures once stood.

Some people did not deserve compassion.

Liza took the silver fabric between her strong fingers and tore.

In her dream, the tearing continued. It was Knot, in dream logic made unremarkably as tall as Liza instead of its usual doll-like stature, seated at the kitchen table tearing her five birthday cards into a small hill of tiny, colorful pieces. As Liza approached, the dream Knot stopped tearing, turned its head, and lifted its chin to face her, its translucent golden face and crudely pinched features curving into a smile. It gestured silently to the shredded cards with its blunt, fingerless hands. Then to the place in its chest where a heart would belong. It raised its brow. As if cut with an invisible blade, a slit began to open in the wax to form a new mouth. Before Knot could speak, Liza awoke.

* * *

Step two. Craft a fabric skeleton out of twisted, plaited strips of cloth, preferably torn from a garment of some significance to the intended target. With beeswax fully liquefied, carefully submerge the skeleton. Hang fully saturated and coated skeleton to cool. When solidified, repeat, dipping and cooling until wax reaches the appropriate thickness for your skeleton's bones. When your frame is complete, allow wax to cool to a temperature that is workable with gloved hands. Fashion your poppet's body to the desired form.

At some unmistakable point in their construction, Liza's sculptures, humanoid or otherwise, took on distinct identities. The curve of a rounded form spoke the language of tree trunks, of pony flanks, of trial and endurance, of patient strength. The partial collapse of a slender tube sighed about vulnerability, about rejection, about loneliness, about loss and the inevitability of decline. This new, larger-than-life-sized poppet spoke, too, in its own silent voice. It spoke of want though its eyes, made of two dull coins pressed into the soft, golden surface of its face. It spoke of disappointment and loss through the wad of shredded birthday cards that hovered, just barely discernible, in the center of its waxen torso where a heart could be.

When Liza felt the quickening of the poppet under her gloved fingers, she paused, remembering a promise made to Althea.

"Knot? Bring me the rope, please."

Knot dropped from the table to the floor with a soft thud and collected a looped length of twisted brown jute. It dropped the rope at Liza's feet.

"My hands are sticky, Knot. Will you tie the poppet's ankle to the table leg, please? We don't want any surprises."

Knot looked from one of its blunt waxen hands to the other as if to say, "Your hands are sticky?" Then it shrugged. With surprising nimbleness, it tethered the poppet to the table by one stout, golden ankle.

Liza draped the poppet in a loose fitting dress from her closet and adjusted a soft, stretchy winter hat on its head. She stepped back to consider her work, then stepped forward again and snugged the cap down lower over the raw, waxen features. The effect would be sufficient in the darkness. All that remained now was to set her creation on its inexorable path.

"Get me a drink, will you, Knot? This calls for a celebration."

Knot retrieved a brown glass bottle from the refrigerator and opened it with ease, flinging the cap into a corner. Liza gazed at the poppet, then raised the beer to her lips and drained half of it.

The phone began to ring. Althea.

Liza silenced the phone.

"Another bottle, Knot."

* * *

Step three. Place an object of personal significance to the intended target into your poppet's hand. Using the index finger of your nondominant hand, create a hole in the side of your poppet's head at the approximate position of an ear. Whisper the name of the intended target to your poppet. Stand clear. The thing is done.

Five brown bottles formed an empty procession across the table when Liza felt the time was right.

The stainless steel Sharp business card was a thing of simple beauty. In the warmth of the kitchen it felt as if it had been kept on ice. It seemed a shame to ruin such a lovely object. Liza turned it over in her hands one last time, running her fingers over the smooth concentric circles and the nubbly texture of the five embossed letters before pushing the metal card deep into the soft wax of the poppet's large hand. A gleaming edge of the card remained visible, glinting in the yellow of the lamplight like a blade.

Liza approached the poppet's side. The figure was so human in form and attitude, relaxing at the kitchen table like a friend, that she felt strange stooping down close to the side of its head, invading its personal space. She raised her left index finger, pointing at the golden figure's head at approximately ear level, then pushed her gloved finger in all the way and withdrew it, rubbing at the resulting stickiness with her other hand. It was a strangely intimate moment, she thought, as she placed her lips close to the hole in the wax and whispered her mouthful of syllables.

The effect was immediate. Liza gasped. She stumbled back as the poppet sprang to its feet, upsetting the chair and knocking the table askew. It swiveled its head slowly left and

right as if getting its bearings, then turned and stared directly at the wall, as if seeing through it into the street. The gaze,
Liza realized, followed a direct line to the lakefront house
and pale rooms of Aimsley Sharp.

Then the poppet paused, as if listening. After a long stillness, its body remained completely motionless as the head
swiveled unnaturally on the golden neck, turning nearly
180 degrees to gaze directly back at Liza. The crude features
showed no expression. The dull coin eyes were lifeless in
their wax hollows. Liza's mind scrabbled for an explanation.
The pajamas she'd used for the skeleton. A bit of her scent
remained in the fabric. Could that be enough to—

The poppet's head abruptly spun again, completing
the 360 degree rotation to face the door, its thick neck now
twisted like an ornamental candle. It began to walk, but was
brought up short and nearly fell as its ankle hit the limit of its
rope tether. Turning its blank, golden gaze to Liza briefly in
mild accusation, the poppet then noticed the glint of metal in
its own hand. In one deft sweeping motion, the poppet bowed
low, severed the rope at the table leg with the steel business
card, and rose to its full height again. With no more hesitation,
it headed to the door. The power of its movements chilled Liza
to the marrow. The thought of what the poppet was capable of,
the memory of its crudely rendered face turning toward her
and locking her in its blank stare filled Liza with horror.

"Knot!" Liza cried, not really knowing what she expected Knot to do. Knot leaped to its feet from its perch on the
tabletop. It looked at Liza, then dropped to the floor, sprinted across the expanse of kitchen floor, and dove to seize the
trailing end of the tether, still attached to the poppet's ankle,
in its doll-sized arms. Holding fast, Knot disappeared along

with the rope through the door as the poppet left to complete its only task.

Liza clung to the refrigerator for support with shaking hands and stared at the open door. The dull sounds of the poppet's footsteps and the familiar thud of the apartment building's door opening and closing faded to an everyday sort of silence. Liza shook her head to clear it, and dove for her phone. One missed call notification appeared on the screen.

Aimsley Sharp.

"Liza! My star! What a treat!" Aimsley said, as if no time had passed at all.

"Mr. Sharp! Where are you?" Liza said.

"Mr. Sharp! What happened to Aims? I'm just finally collapsing here at the lake house with a glass of wine and my niece, Lola. We've had a hell of a few weeks. Family drama. Say hello, Lola!" Aims said. It clearly wasn't his first glass of wine. Liza heard a female voice in the background, but couldn't make out the words.

"Your niece?" Liza said.

"Long story short she's left school. Her mother will probably slaughter me for going to collect her, but what the hell? I like being the cool uncle, so I'm letting her crash with me for a while. She's even decided to pick up some paint brushes, so I've given her my available studio space for the time being. But don't panic— I've got a couple of deadbeats who aren't producing up to Sharp standards, so you'll have your choice of spots within the week. Then we can start getting ready for that Venice trip. Have you had a chance to do any wardrobe shopping?"

Liza's kitchen tilted on its axis.

"Aims, listen to me. You need to leave," Liza said. "You need to get out of the house, do you hear me? Take your niece and get out, go anywhere, but you need to leave now!"

"What are you talking about, Liza star? Oop—hang on a minute. There's someone at the door. Lola, can you get that?"

Liza dropped the phone and ran.

As Liza dropped her scooter and made her gasping, trembling way through the darkness up the long, meandering private drive to the lake house, the glowing windows seemed to offer a possibility of hope. The last turn through the trees brought her close enough to see how misleading the glow was. The front door stood open. Within, golden light spilled over toppled furniture, shattered ceramics, and pale walls splashed with bright color. One bright color. The silence was absolute. Liza took in a long breath, thinking she might call out to someone inside. Before she formed the words, Knot's dull staccato footsteps broke the stillness, beating a rhythm from the open door all the way to her feet.

"Knot? You okay?" Liza asked weakly.

Knot craned its head back to look up at Liza and nodded with enthusiasm, its twine topknot bouncing. It raised its hands up to show Liza the reddened Sharp business card, clutched between two waxy golden arms festooned with embedded shreds of the rope tether and a few wildly kinky long hairs. Knot had managed to disarm the poppet, but the thing was done. There was no undoing it now. She filled her lungs with the thick, sweet forest air and with a ragged sound, sighed it out.

"Good job, Knot. Good job. Thank you," Liza said.

* * *

Step four. When your poppet's task is complete, remove the object of personal significance from its hand. Discard it from your possession and discard the memory from your mind. May you never use these instructions again.

Liza walked to the water's edge and threw the Sharp business card as hard as she could. It twirled and glinted in the air, skipped three times across the lake's surface and disappeared.

"Come on, Knot," Liza said. "Let's get out of here." She raised her shoulders to her ears and let them fall, rolling them a few times. She shook all over, as if coming in from a sudden downpour. She bent low, scooped Knot up with one motion, and placed it on her shoulder. "We can't let these losses and setbacks get the better of us, Knot. Althea's right. We've got to pick ourselves up, dust ourselves off, and get on with the business of living. We've got art to make." They disappeared into the shadows.

* * *

On the shore of Lake Washington, the Aimsley and Lola Aurora Sharp Memorial Sculpture Park is a must-see for visitors to Seattle with an interest in art. Created after the demolition of the Sharp home, the park features one of the largest collections of contemporary outdoor sculptures in the United States and is situated on several wooded acres of prime lakefront property. No plants are cultivated in order to minimize both distraction from the beauty of the sculptures and the unusual enthusiasm of the local honeybees, which in the past have invaded the park to the exclusion of human visitors.

Aimsley Sharp's unmatched private collection includes works by many of the most acclaimed artists of the 20th and early 21st centuries, including a small, select group of local artists discovered on the streets of Seattle by Mr. Sharp himself and elevated to world renown in his ceaseless search for examples of perfection in form and expression. Mr. Sharp is no longer with us. Long may his vision endure.

CHANGING GABE

Kathrine Stewart

It's no fun being trapped in a fourteen-by-six-foot camper van. At least today I had a distraction.

I traced my finger over the pictures on the diary cover— unicorns and rainbows, just my style. But it didn't belong to me, and there's an unwritten rule, you don't read someone else's diary. Not a rule to break lightly, especially for someone like me. My ears twitched at the mere thought of the consequences.

So, I couldn't read the diary, but how else was I meant to find out who it belonged to? Classic Catch-22. I licked my finger and drew a no-entry sign in the air above the book, just to be safe; my curiosity had a mind of its own and tended to rope in the rest of me. Not my worst trait apparently— according to Gabe, that was my mischievousness, and it was also the cause of my current living conditions. You'd think a girl was allowed a little fun, but no. *Bloody consequences.*

I abandoned the diary on the bench seat and went to sit in the front, feet up on the furry purple dashboard, jangling the bells that hung from the rear-view mirror with my toes. Gabe hated the décor—the psychedelic colours, the scented candles and homemade charms, but I was the one stuck in here. Perhaps I should switch on the fairy lights to annoy him.

He was down by the lake, swatting mosquitoes while he waited for the contact. His six-and-a-half-foot frame, clothed in a too-white-shirt and black trousers that hugged his butt like they were spray painted on, was hard to miss. The whole chiselled jaw and dark eyes made people stare. I told him it was his bad dress sense, but we both knew that wasn't true.

Above his head, pale in the daytime sky, was the moon, like a damn halo. Had he stood there on purpose? Probably not. But I didn't believe in coincidences, either. The moon had an aura, just like the circle I'd drawn over the diary, but with no Keep Out line scored through it. Was there significance in that? Just then a crow flew across the sky, left to right, and as it passed the moon, it looked at me and cawed. Replay what I said about coincidences. I gave the bells an extra hard jangle to dispel the prickles that crawled over my skin.

A man had joined Gabe. He wasn't much more than a kid, really. Gabe said a few words, then handed over the package I'd prepared. The boy hugged it to his chest and smiled. Job done, and another happy customer. I should be pleased. We could finally get out of here, but that damn diary was taunting me.

As Gabe walked back from the lake, a black cat sauntered up to him. Of course, he bent down to stroke it. I banged on the windscreen to stop him, but he rolled his eyes and carried on petting it. How many times had I told him not to? Black cats are tricky creatures; you never can tell if they're good or bad luck. I crossed my fingers and blew on them.

That was three portents in as many minutes—good reason to be nervous. I glanced over my shoulder at the diary. You'd think someone was trying to send me a message, but that wasn't in my job description. I solved problems as punishment for my screwy sense of humour; Gabe was the messenger. Still, the signs were telling me something. Not to mention my whole curiosity thing.

The back of the van lurched and dropped three inches as Gabe climbed in. He wasn't exactly smiling, but his usual po-faced expression was as close to pleased as it could get.

"Time to move on, Pix," he said.

He really was too big for this van, swamping the space with his broad shoulders. Good thing I was so small. I clambered into the back and sat cross-legged on the seat, settling orange gauze skirts over green leggings and fingering the glittering pouch at my waist. "I'm not so sure."

Gabe's eyes snapped to mine. "What's that meant to mean? Our task is completed and it's time to get going."

It would be easy to agree, and I wanted to. Outside the sun and sky beckoned, a breeze rippled the branches of the trees and birds flitted with a freedom I ached for, but the signs were telling me something. My gaze slid to the diary.

"Not that book again, Pix. I'm regretting ever picking it up."

But he had. And he'd given it to me, so now I couldn't ignore it.

"It was meant to keep you from annoying me. I should have known you'd take it as one of your signs." He leaned toward me to add weight to his words. "Forget this superstitious codswallop. It's time to go."

"That's your opinion." I folded my arms.

He clenched his teeth and summoned his best glare: eyes narrowed, face in full scowl mode. I smiled sweetly.

"We're going," he growled and climbed into the front.

"You can't drive this thing without me." I pointed out.

Muscles rippled under his shirt, but he let out a slow breath and stared up at the sky. He was doing that thing—centering himself, finding his inner calm. I called it bloody irritating.

"You're forgetting I'm more patient than you, Pix. I can wait."

He settled in the driver's seat, hands resting lightly on the steering wheel, eyes closed. Looking bleeding angelic. Well, maybe butterflies did have a longer attention span than me, but there was something important about this diary. Luckily, I was the queen of annoying. Time to hum. *The Birdie Song, Achy Breaky Heart, Barbie Girl, Doop Doop*. It took two hours, but Gangnam style finally broke him.

He launched himself into the back with a roar that had me twitching, snatched up the diary, and hurled it at the door. It arced through the air, light and sparkles trailing from its pages like a mini rainbow, and Gabe's jaw dropped. He crept to the book, crouched down and touched its cover.

After a moment his shoulders relaxed. "Just glitter."

I snickered. "What were you expecting, magic?"

That got me a foul look, and he slammed the book on the table, still open at the place where it had fallen. The first page. There was a little flutter in my stomach. I hadn't opened the book, so surely this didn't count as rule breaking—it would be ok to read. I leaned closer. A name: Lucy Fenning, and an address.

I laid a finger on the writing and raised an eyebrow.

Gabe scowled. "I threw the book and it opened. That's what books do. There's no special message in there, Pix."

"Are you certain of that?"

"We follow official instructions only."

God, was he a stickler. "Come on, Gabe. Aren't you all about the good deeds? Just one tiny message. Go tell her we found it."

He rolled his eyes to the ceiling and he was definitely counting to ten, or maybe fifteen hundred.

"You're not going to give me any peace, are you?"

I smiled.

"Fine. Hand it over."

"What? No!" I put myself between him and it. "The signs show I was meant to—"

He growled but I stood my ground; even if he could pick me up with one hand, the book had come to me for a reason. Finally, he shook his head and left without it.

The door slammed and the pages rippled in the current. Would they turn? I held my breath and leaned closer. No such luck, but it gave me an idea. Why not open a window or two?

The first caused a faint movement in the air, but the second set up a cross wind. The pages flapped, settled, flapped again. And turned. I pounced, flattening them. This was an invitation to read. It had to be.

I took a deep breath and drew the book onto my lap.

It started out mundane enough. School gossip and make-up tips, gripes about parents and thoughts on the cutest boy at school. But as the pages turned the memories became darker. An argument, a broken friendship, tears in the girls' toilets. Then came the snide words and the bullying. Lucy's pain screeched at me from the pages. If I wasn't here for this, what was I here for?

The clonk as the door opened startled me to the present. Gabe was back. But delivering a message shouldn't leave him looking like this. His face was bleached white, jaw set, as he stumbled, in a very un-Gabe like way, into the van.

"You were right." His hands trembled as he dropped onto the seat.

I slowly closed the diary and peered into his face. "What happened?"

"She was on a bridge."

"A bridge?" He wasn't making sense.

"She was going to jump."

"Oh," I breathed. "What did you do?"

He swallowed and ran a hand through his hair. "I... I stopped her. Told her to come here."

My mouth opened and shut but nothing came out. Unusual for me, I know. But this was the thing, Gabe always did things by the book. Passing a message to Lucy that we'd found her diary was a small matter, but stepping in like that, exercising his vast magnetism to stop her without being told to. For Gabe that was a huge deal. No wonder he was rattled. And yet, sometimes I wondered about him.

He was the big kahuna. The message carrier. And here he was, in a camper van, running errands with me. They were important errands, in a small way—important to the people we helped, but nothing like the tasks he used to do. I'd always thought his job was to keep me in line, but maybe he wasn't in favor, either.

I put my hands on his shoulders and looked into his eyes. "You did the right thing, Gabriel."

He gave a low laugh. "Coming from you, Pix, I doubt that's true. And now I've acted, you're going to have to help her."

I pursed my lips. This was more than returning a lost diary, and that wasn't something I'd planned for. I opened a cupboard and sorted through bottles of coloured liquids, bunches of dried herbs and pots of shimmering powder. The scent of cinnamon and vanilla prickled my nose as I picked up and discarded items: a rose crystal, a piece of amber, an iridescent feather that I'd found under a full moon. Nothing felt right.

"This is serious," Gabe said. "One of your idiotic charms won't work. You need something big."

Idiotic! What did he think was in all the packages he delivered? Would this morning's customer be complaining when my charm lifted his mother's sadness? Humph. I'd give him idiotic. My hand hovered over a pot of powdered poison ivy; a flick of that down the back of his shirt would show him. And if it got in his feathers, it'd be hell to get out.

But he was right about this, and I guessed what he meant me to do—I just didn't want to.

I snapped the cupboard shut, putting the poison ivy out of temptation's way, and drummed my fingers on the wood. "You know Titania and I aren't talking."

Gabe snorted. "Surely you're not still feuding."

"Still!" My voice came out as a squeak. "She's the reason I'm stuck here."

"No, Pix." His face took on that patient, sanctimonious look that drove me nuts. "You're here because of one of your pranks. There were a lot of red faces the day the 'Fairies at the Bottom of the Garden' story hit the newspapers. Titania was furious and nobody thought it was funny."

"Fine," I muttered.

He couldn't help but rub my face in it. And it had been funny. If his kind could stop acting as if they had spikes stuck up their butts for just a moment, they might have seen the funny side, too. There again, would their faces crack if they smiled? A theory to test in the future, but right now I had to help Lucy.

There must be another way than asking Titania for help. Maybe I should try conjuring a genie in a bottle? Not something I'd attempted before, but there's a first time for everything. Gabe was watching me, waiting. Dammit, he was right. There was no time to experiment—I'd have to persuade Titania, but how?

I took out my favourite goose feather quill and lavender ink, my fairy stone, and a box of matches. Perhaps Lucy's words could get Titania's attention. Whispering an apology, I tore a page from the diary and scribbled my message in the margin. I clenched the fairy stone in my hand, muttered Titania's name three times and struck a match.

"Pix, what are you doing?"

"Shhh."

I held the page to the flame. The edge caught, curled, then ignited with a rush.

"Message sent, and fingers crossed that she's listening."

Gabe waved his phone under my nose. "All you had to do was call her. Your silly rituals..."

My glare stopped him and he shook his head.

"Forget it, I'll call her myself." But he paused, phone

halfway to his ear, gaze fixed across the carpark. "Too late. Lucy is here. You're going to have to sort this on your own."

He jumped out of the van, leaving the door open, and walked away. It was still daylight, but as he passed under a carpark lamp it came on, bathing his head in a halo of radiance, just like the moon earlier. I shivered. Another sign.

Mostly, they were as clear as swamp water, but just occasionally I *knew*, and this one's meaning slipped into me with a crystal certainty. I gave an unsteady laugh. None of the signs had been about the diary, but about Gabe. He needed to learn to do things because they were right, not because he'd been told to. That was why he'd been put with me. That was my mission and the way to win my freedom. Boy, was he going to hate this.

But first there was Lucy. My charms might not be enough to solve her problems but every little helped. I slipped a sliver of birch bark, for new beginnings, into the spine of the diary, and a sprig of forget-me-knot between the pages for a touch of magnetism. Now Lucy just had to accept the gift, and the rest was up to Titania.

Leaving the book on the table, I put the kettle on and laid out cups. Lucy was taking her time, but she'd find me eventually; saying no to Gabe was nigh on impossible.

"Hello?" Her voice from outside the van was wary.

"Hello, you must be Lucy." I touched the diary.

"Ye-es." She took a step closer and peered at the book.

"I found it on a bench. Thought you might want it back."

"Right. Thanks." She held out her hand.

But that wasn't going to work—she was too far away. I wasn't allowed out of the van, not even by a hair's breadth, so she might as well have been on the other side of the world.

I could lob the diary at her, but that didn't exactly fit with the spirit of gift acceptance. Plus, with my dodgy throwing skills, I'd probably end up blacking her eye. No, she was going to have to pick it up herself.

"Camomile tea?" I suggested, not waiting for an answer before pouring.

She glanced around the car park and shuffled her feet. What was holding her back? The lucky horseshoes hanging over the door usually persuaded everybody in. Maybe they needed a polish. I sat down and took a sip of tea. *Come on Lucy, I'm hardly intimidating.*

After a few moments the van shifted as she climbed in.

She fiddled with the zip of her hoodie while staring at the diary as if it might leap up and bite her. "I'm not sure I want it back."

Typical. Things were never straightforward. I shrugged as if it didn't matter and took another sip of tea.

She settled opposite me and looked around. "Nice van."

"Thanks." At least somebody had taste.

"Do you travel a lot?"

I hid a smile behind my cup. "You could say that."

She picked up one of my more experimental scented candles, gave it a sniff and wrinkled her nose. As she set it back on the table there was the shimmer of tears in her eyes. Somehow, I doubted they were caused by the smell.

"I'd like this kind of freedom," she said.

Well, that was ironic, but there was something I'd learnt from being stuck in here, and that I could share. A little wisdom that might help her. "The best freedom's inside your head."

She looked thoughtful. Gabe says I could talk a leprechaun

out of his pot of gold, but sometimes silence is more healing. I let Lucy sip her tea and think.

When she finally stood, she gave me a nod and turned to the door.

Not so fast. I tapped the diary. If she didn't take it, Titania would never find her.

She hovered for a moment, looking at the book, then shrugged and picked it up. "Thanks."

I let out a slow breath. The gift had been accepted, but looking to see if it had worked might be bad luck, so I closed my eyes and whistled. Only when the van sank several inches, announcing Gabe's return, did I crack open one eye.

"Well?" I asked.

"I don't know how you managed it, but..."

Oh no, he wasn't going to get away with that. I looked for something pointy to throw at him, but had to settle for a cushion. Maybe now he would believe in my charms. "So, we did the right thing, then?"

He frowned, but only for a moment. "Yes, we did the right thing."

I threw a mental high five. Round one in the Change Gabriel Cup goes to Pix. But this was just the beginning—would next time be so easy?

I gave myself a shake. "Can we go now?"

Gabe chuckled and climbed into the front. "Now you're impatient!"

He turned the key, the engine growled to life, and freedom beckoned. I touched the barrier between the van and the outside. It rippled against my fingertips. A moment's concentration was all it took to draw together light and colour.

"Rainbow's forming," Gabe shouted from the front.

Of course it was bloody forming. I wasn't an amateur.

I leaned farther out and the van vibrated, bucking and snorting like a bronco. Sparks spat from the exhaust pipe and the lights flashed.

"For goodness sakes, Pix," Gabe yelled. "People are staring. Throw the Pixie dust."

And they were—Lucy among them. To my eyes, there was a shimmer on her shoulder—a fairy godmother of her very own, whispering beautiful possibilities in her ear. I suppose I was going to have to thank Titania.

"Where are we needed next?" I called.

"We'll find out soon enough. Get on with it."

Grinning, I dipped my hand into my pouch and drew out dust that gleamed and glittered on my fingertips. A flick, and it shimmered into the air, confounding the eyes of anyone watching.

I drew in a breath, tasting the colours of the rainbow. It stretched away, beckoning me to ride the currents of a more wonderful world. It was time to pass the threshold and become a pixie again. With a laugh, I rocketed into the open, caught the tail of the rainbow and threw us into the air.

LIKE THE BRIGHT MOON
(WE STILL HAVE OUR DARKER SIDE)

Kelsey Wheaton

East London—April 1971

Rowan tried not to look suspicious as he strolled down the almost-empty sidewalk, squinting at street signs. He'd plotted a path on a cheap map of the city that he'd picked up at the bus station, but of course, he'd left it on the bed at the run-down hotel he was staying at in Tower Hamlets. He knew there were parks that were much closer to where he was staying, including a cemetery park right off the Mile End Tube station. But Epping Forest was an actual, honest-to-God forest where he could go lose himself for a few hours. Besides that, the idea of running through a cemetery, even one that had been made into a public park, made his skin crawl. The convenience wasn't worth accidentally pissing off any restless spirits that might have still been skulking about.

He'd gotten off the Tube at Loughton, knowing that his window of opportunity was limited. The last train left

Loughton at eleven-thirty, and if he wasn't on it, then he'd be walking his sorry ass back to Tower Hamlets, no matter how worn out he was. He checked his watch. It was just past eight. That gave him three hours to have his fun, then get dressed and make for the station and hopefully have time to spare.

A pair of teenagers were sitting on a nearby bench, entwined with each other. The girl was facing him; she whispered something in her boyfriend's ear, and he turned to look Rowan up and down with a judgmental sneer.

Rowan scowled. "What? You never seen a bloke out for a late-night jog?"

Both teens' eyes went wide when Rowan called them out, and they slunk off the bench, disappearing across the street. Rowan sighed. He knew he looked like a mess, with his dingy, second-hand jogging suit and ratty trainers that he'd picked up at a charity shop, but he wasn't about to risk the halfway-decent shirts and jeans he did own. He'd lost or destroyed enough clothing over the years to know better.

Besides, he was taking the damn thing off when he got to the park, anyways.

Although there were no gates around Epping Forest, Rowan was still cautious as he approached one of the trailheads. Any police officers nearby might find it suspicious that he was sneaking into the forest after dark, and, well ... if they followed him, he had no idea how to explain what they would see. But he couldn't see anyone, and, weak as the sense was in this form, he couldn't smell anyone, either. So he jogged down the trailhead, plunging into the darkness offered by the trees.

Once he was sure that he was far enough in not to be spotted from the road, Rowan slowed to a walk, looking for a spot to stop and discard his jogging suit—and a place he would remember at the end of the night, because a naked man on the Tube would cause much more of a stir than a man in old workout clothes. He came across a clearing with trees dotted about and a ditch that circled a series of hills and low banks, too uniform to be natural. A plaque had been placed at the edge of the ditch, and he stopped to read it. The place was called Loughton Camp, and it had been a fortress back in the Iron Age. There wasn't anything left of the place now, though, not even the foundation, but it wasn't much of a stretch to imagine the kinds of battles that might have happened here. A shiver ran through him, and his blood thrummed under his skin.

There was a tree about five steps away. It was memorable enough for him. He toed off his shoes, bundling his socks inside of them and nudging them to the base of the tree. His watch went into the pocket of the jacket, then he unzipped his jacket, dropping the ugly, dull orange thing in a pile on top of his shoes. He shucked off his T-shirt and dropped it onto the pile. He hooked his thumbs into the waistband of his joggers, and, in one fluid and well-practiced motion, pulled them and his underwear down in one movement, kicking them into the pile. Naked as the day he was born, he stood, shivering in the evening chill, and flexed the fingers of his left hand. The knuckle joints swelled, and the creeping itchiness beneath his skin told him hair was sprouting thick and dark across the back of his hands and fingers. He grit his teeth as his stubby, chewed fingernails grew impossibly fast, becoming three-inch claws with wickedly sharp tips. Rowan lashed out, ripping four jagged gouges into the bark of the tree, grinning at the savage pleasure of it. The feeling of wood splintering and shredding under his nails sent a rush of adrenaline through him. The knot of scar tissue on his thigh burned fever-hot.

He threw his head back and surrendered to the primal urge of the Change.

He had to try not to howl as the pain took him to his knees. Beneath his skin, bones cracked and shifted, contorting his body into a shape that was neither human nor animal, but somewhere in between. He wheezed in pain as the bones in his leg grew, adding height to his frame inch by agonizing inch. Claws dug deep into the dirt as his rib cage expanded to make room for his growing lungs. His heart pumped hard enough that it seemed likely to burst from his chest. Human moans of pain gave way to whines and growls as his nose and mouth pushed out of his face, growing together into a snout not suited for human speech. Coarse fur, black in the moonlight that streamed through the treetops, grew in patches across his body, feeling like thousands of tiny, white-hot needles punching through his skin.

When it was all said and done, Rowan lay on the forest floor panting, ignoring the hard roots of the trees that dug into his stomach. Though the Change had only taken a minute, it had still felt like a lifetime as he went from *human* to *not*.

To *more than*.

He lifted his head. The smell of the night was clearer now, made sharp by the scent of the forest animals around. His ears twitched as squirrels chattered overhead. His nose wrinkled as a rabbit scurried through the underbrush. He could smell a deer in the mix, too, and his stomach rumbled at the thought. He hadn't eaten dinner, and fresh, raw venison was a far cry from the soggy fish and chips he'd scarfed down for lunch.

The pain had faded. He got to all fours—though he could walk upright on two legs, as well—and took off into the trees, losing himself to the thrill of the chase.

Rowan Walsh was gone. Only the wolf remained.

***

The deer had given him the slip somewhere in the trees, but the hunt wasn't a total wash. Rowan had found two plump rabbits and made dinner of them instead, and now he plodded back towards Loughton Camp, satisfied. It was good to get out of his skin for a while. Though he was no longer forced into the Change by the full moon, he was always more restless and peevish when the moon was full—and had gotten into a lot of fights on both sides of the Iron Curtain because of it. Being in London, with nothing to occupy his days, had only made the restless feeling worse. Epping Forest had been a godsend.

At the edge of a swath of forest was an open field of tall grass, and a pond, moonlight glinting off its silvery surface. It would probably be a good idea to stop at the pond and clean up. There was rabbit blood drying in his fur and on his claws that he should wash off before he made it back onto the Tube. He slipped from the trees, into the open field, but then froze.

Something was crouched at the edge of the pond, oblivious to its surroundings as it drank. Rowan licked his chops. If it was the deer that had given him the slip earlier, then to Hell with the Tube—he'd stay here and glut himself on venison and walk back to Tower Hamlets. He crouched low, slinking forward, continually glancing back and forth from his feet to the prize at the water's edge. The night was calm, with no wind to speak of. The ground was soft, but not sticky, and there was nothing he could step on that would make noise, no errant branches or dead leaves. With any luck, his prey wouldn't know he was there until he was right on top of it.

The creature at the edge of the lake lifted its head. A pair of tufted ears twitched, listening, and Rowan froze.

Deer didn't have tufted ears.

The creature stood, rising to a full seven-plus feet on two legs. It turned toward Rowan, golden eyes gleaming. Blood dripped from a mouthful of yellowed canines. It snarled, ears flattening against its lupine skull. Rowan knew the sound was a warning, a sign that it would be in his best interest to turn tail and run, but he stayed, gaping in disbelief at the sight before him.

It was another werewolf.

Thirty years of traveling across Europe, and Rowan had only ever seen one other werewolf—and if he ever saw the face of the gaunt sack of shit who had Turned him again, it would be too soon. He'd known he couldn't have been the only one on the continent. During the war, there'd been rumors of deaths too gruesome to even be the work of Nazis, bodies left torn open and mutilated on battlefields. Afterwards, it had been attacks on farms, or travelers who went missing off of desolate stretches of motorways, never to be seen again. But while he had heard rumors and caught whiffs of scents, he hadn't actually seen hide nor hair of another werewolf, excluding his sire, since he'd been bitten.

Another growl. Behind the werewolf, he could see the

carcass of the deer that had escaped him earlier. Its entire chest cavity was open, bloodied ribs cracked open to get at the entrails. Rowan huffed, disappointed.

Lucky bastard.

It was clear that the other werewolf wasn't in the mood for sharing or having company. Rowan took a step to the side, then another, hoping the other would get his message: *I'm not staying. I'll leave you alone.* He wasn't scared of the possibility of a fight; the other werewolf may have been male, but he was smaller than Rowan. But it would just be better if it didn't come to a fight.

A third growl, and there was teeth with this one. Either the other werewolf was terrible at reading body language, or he *really* hated Rowan. Annoyed, he flashed his teeth and growled back.

Bad idea.

The werewolf snarled at him, hackles raised and hatred in his yellow eyes. He reared back, then pounced, clearing ten feet. His front feet hit the ground, and he charged Rowan. Accepting his challenge, Rowan ran to meet him. Surely, one or two good cuffs would put the upstart little bastard in his place and send him running with his tail between his legs.

They collided in a tangle of teeth and claws. The other male may have been smaller, but he was fast: a snap here, a flash of claws there. A slash to Rowan's chest. Teeth snapping in his face. Biting, growling, claws red with blood. Rowan could barely keep up. He snapped back. Growled. Kicked the male in the chest to break free. Sank teeth into the male's shoulder, the taste of blood exploding on his tongue. The male punched him in the side of his face, and he let go, reeling, spitting a mouthful of bloody drool onto the ground.

The male growled, then pounced onto Rowan's back, intent on round two.

They rolled across the ground, biting and snapping. Clods of dirt and fistfuls of grass flew as they attacked and missed. Blood filled Rowan's mouth, matted into his fur. Somewhere deep inside, the part of Rowan's brain that had remained human begged him to stop the fight, to think about the fact that this other creature was a man, too. He knew it would be best for both of them if they just stopped fighting and went their separate ways. But he was running on instinct now, and all he wanted to do was put the bastard in his place.

Finally, he got an opening. The other male had left his entire right side unprotected. Rowan lunged with impossibly wide jaws, clamping down. A rib snapped under the pressure of Rowan's bite, the sound like a gunshot in his ears. Blood gushed into his mouth. He gave the other werewolf a savage thrash, then let go, sending him sprawling into the grass. Triumph made his blood rush, pounding in his head. He snapped at the smaller male with bloody teeth, daring him to make another move.

Next time, it'll be your throat.

The smaller male froze, ears twitching. The sound of feet and breaking twigs reached Rowan's ears. They both turned, and saw flashlight beams bobbing through the woods. A shrill whistle shattered the still night air. Either they had been patrolling the park and had heard the noise, or the fight had been so loud that someone had called, but either way, the cops were heading for them, and there was no good way to explain what was going on.

The other male got up. One large, furry, clawed hand clutched at his side, where Rowan had bitten him. Blood seeped between his fingers to splatter on the ground. Pained yellow eyes met Rowan's, and a twinge of guilt twisted through his gut. Avoiding the human cops was going to be a hell of a lot harder for that poor bugger if he was leaving a trail behind. Before Rowan could do anything, however, the other male dropped into a crouch, staggering toward the tree line, blood dripping into the dirt from his side.

The cops were getting closer, not even bothering to be quiet about their approach. The grass of the meadows was tall, but not enough for Rowan to disappear. He dropped to all fours anyways, sprinting for the cover of the woods he'd come from.

If the cops wanted a chase, well then, he would lead them on a merry one.

***

The cops eventually gave up the search, panting and cursing Rowan six ways to Sunday for the four-mile chase through the woods he'd taken them on. They finally called it quits near Loughton Camp, stalking back up the path toward town, grumbling about teenagers playing pranks. As soon as the sounds of their footsteps faded away, Rowan climbed down into the camp. He'd made it to the site with just enough time to snatch up his abandoned clothes and scurry up the closest tree. He'd spent nearly half an hour balancing precariously on a tree branch, trying not to move for fear of making his presence known to the cops.

As soon as his feet touched the ground, he let the Change sweep back over him. He'd gotten into enough trouble for one night.

Going back to human wasn't as painful as going full wolf, but it still took Rowan to his knees, groaning and swearing once his mouth returned to a shape suited for human speech. His fur fell out in clumps, still matted with blood, and his fingers bled as his claws retracted into his nail beds. He felt like a rag that had been wrung out, drained of strength and energy, but he couldn't afford to lay down on the ground and recover. Both the fight and the chase had cost him precious time, and he'd be lucky if he made it onto the train.

He yanked the ugly jogging suit back on, not even caring when he realized he'd put his trousers on backwards. As soon as he'd shoved his feet into his shoes, he took off down the trail. Stray low-hanging branches snagged at his clothing, and he tripped on his untied shoelaces constantly, but he ignored it all and kept running, bursting out of Epping Forest like all of Hell was on his heels.

The streets were empty. Up ahead, he could see the lights of the Tube station's platform, beckoning him to his destination. A dull gray-green train idled on the tracks, and Rowan's heart leapt at the sight of it.

As he charged up to the station's entrance, however, he heard the familiar hiss of air brakes releasing. His eyes went wide.

"No no no no no no!"

He jumped the turnstiles and ran flat-out for the stairs. The station attendant yelled after him, but he ignored the man, taking the steps up to the platform two at a time. He was too late, he knew he was too late, but he refused to believe it. If he could just jump onto one of the car connectors, or even grab the rails at the back of the train ... it wouldn't be a safe ride, and it certainly wouldn't be comfortable, but Rowan had done far more stupid things and had lived to tell the tale. If balancing on a car connector or clinging to the back of a train would spare him the twenty-kilometer walk of shame back to Tower Hamlets, then he'd do it.

The train was almost to the end of the platform by the time he made it up. He sprinted after it, feeling like his lungs might pop. Even werewolf endurance had a limit, and Rowan had reached his.

Four cars still within the bounds of the platform. He put on a burst of speed.

Three cars left. He reached out his hand, desperate, grasping.

Two cars left. He could make it...

One car left. He *had* to make it...

The end of the last car cleared the platform, and Rowan skidded to a hard halt to keep from going over the edge and onto the tracks. There had been maybe a foot between his hand and the car before it had cleared the platform. The train disappeared into the darkness, red brake lights teasing him. He flopped down onto the platform, barely registering the pain of slamming his tailbone into the poured concrete.

"Well *fuck*."

***

Rowan had only been awake for an hour, and already he wanted to crawl back into his hotel bed. The only reason he'd bothered waking up and making himself look somewhat presentable was because he was starving.

Literally missing the train by thirty seconds had only been the beginning of last night's troubles. The station attendant had come up onto the platform after him, still yelling about him having jumped the turnstiles, going so far as to threaten to call the police. He had managed to placate the man by literally shoving all the money he'd had in his pockets into the man's palm, then walked out of the station and hit the streets. He'd walked the twenty kilometers back to his hotel in Tower Hamlets, and it had taken him almost the whole night. By the time he'd arrived back at his room, he was so exhausted that he didn't even bother with a shower or taking off his dirty clothes. He'd flopped down on the bed and passed out.

He'd dreamed about the other werewolf. Dreamed of fighting him again, tearing not into the wolf's side, but his throat—only to step back and see the flesh of a man, torn and bleeding. He'd dreamed of the werewolf being taken alive by those cops that had chased him. Of scalpels slicing into fur and skin, dissecting him under the harshness of fluorescent lights. And then it had become him on a cold steel lab table, being taken apart in the name of science. He'd dreamed of the police finding the werewolf and putting a bullet through his skull, leaving him to die alone in the forest. He'd dreamed of Farrow, the only other survivor after his sire attacked his platoon, the morning after they'd both made their first Change. Watched as Farrow had put the barrel of his pistol into his mouth and pulled the trigger. Even with thirty years between them, Farrow's face merged with that of the unnamed werewolf.

Had that werewolf been left dead and forgotten in Epping Forest the way he'd had to leave Farrow behind?

He shook his head. Dead or alive, there was no chance he'd see the other werewolf again. Even if he'd made it out of Epping Forest, London was a city of seven million people. The fact that they'd met once had been a miracle in and of itself, but twice? Rowan would have had better luck with a needle in a haystack.

He stopped in front of a hole-in-the-wall pub with opaque glass windows. A warm, yellow glow came from within, a welcome sight in the damp, cold rain, and Rowan made for the door, yanking it open. The smell of cooking grease and human sweat greeted him.

And something else.

He stepped inside, letting the door fall closed behind him, and sniffed again. He'd thought it was a mistake at first, but now that he was inside, he could definitely smell it: the distinct musk of a werewolf, too subtle for humans to smell, but not enough to escape his nose, even in human form.

And not just any werewolf.

The same werewolf he'd fought the night before.

Son of a bitch, he marveled. *He made it out.*

He scanned the bar with narrowed eyes. There were only a few ladies in the bar, which didn't really narrow down his choices much. A few tables were taken, their occupants sharing plates of soggy appetizers. None of the blokes at the tables really struck Rowan as werewolves, but he still picked his way through toward the bar, sniffing discreetly.

All of them were human, so he turned his attention to the bar, instead. There was a large group of gents crowded at one end of the bar, clapping each other on the back, clinking pint glasses together, and singing loudly to "Hot Love" as it played from the radio mounted behind the bar. Rowan lingered at the outside of their group, pretending to study the taps while sniffing. They were all human, too, to his disappointment.

"Your usual."

Out of the corner of his eye, Rowan spotted the bartender setting an entire bottle of whiskey and a shot glass down in front of one patron: a man sitting at the corner of the L-shaped bar, with dark, shoulder-length hair and a full beard to match. He didn't even look up from the battered paperback he was reading, just handed the bartender a twenty.

"Keep the change," he said quietly.

He got up, strolling casually toward the end of the bar. The musky smell got stronger as he moved toward the man. It took everything to keep the smirk off his face.

Gotcha.

He stopped at the stool nearest to the man, glancing down at the empty seat and then back up. After a moment, the man looked up from his book, and Rowan flashed him a winning smile.

"Mind if I sit over here? It's a bit crowded down that way," he asked, jerking his thumb at the blokes down on the other end of the bar.

"Go ahead." His attention went back to his book as Rowan plopped onto the stool next to him. This close, there was no mistaking it: this was the same werewolf he met last night. Rowan had to admit, he was a little impressed—his sire had been just as awful-looking in his human skin as he had in his fur, but this man was actually kind of handsome, if a little shaggy-looking. He wondered if the man could smell him. If the man had scented him as soon as he'd stepped into the bar. If he had, he was either playing it cool or biding his time and waiting to attack again. Given how he'd torn into Rowan last night, he'd put what little money he had on the latter.

"You know, I don't think I've ever seen anyone reading in a bar," Rowan commented, propping his chin on his t hand. "Why come out here to read? It's drier at home."

"This is how I socialize."

"Hate to be rude, mate, but ... you're not really socializing."

The man lowered his book slightly, raising an eyebrow. Rowan's stomach did an unexpected somersault as he got a good look at the man's eyes. They were a gorgeous shade of blue-gray, like the sea after a storm.

"I'm talking to you, aren't I?"

Rowan couldn't help but chuckle. "I suppose you are. But ... are we really socializing? I mean, you're reading and I'm sitting next to you, that's not really being social. I don't even know your name."

The man looked up from his book again, and Rowan was certain this was the part where he'd either snap on him, or, to avoid causing a commotion in the bar, tell him to piss off and go bother someone else. But the corner of the man's mouth twitched up into the barest hint of a smile, and Rowan's heart missed a beat.

"Elias."

"Huh?"

"My name. It's Elias."

"Oh! Elias. Yeah. Great name. Nice." He swallowed, trying not to cringe at how dumb he sounded. "I'm Rowan."

Elias nodded, then set his book down, opening the whiskey and pouring some into the glass. He slid the bottle over to Rowan. "I'm not going to drink it all, so you're welcome to some."

Well, damn. He was a lot nicer out of his fur, too. Rowan offered him a smile.

"Thanks, mate. Cheers."

Elias nodded, then took down his whiskey in one go. As he tilted his head back, Rowan noticed a bit of scar tissue peeking out of the collar of his shirt, right about where his neck met his shoulder. An odd place for an injury, but the perfect spot for a werewolf bite.

"So," Rowan began, reaching over the bar counter to grab a shot glass. "you come here often?"

"Couple times a week. I live just around the corner. You sound like you're not from around here."

"Manchester, born and raised."

"I'll try not to hold it against you," Elias said with one of those little smiles. Rowan's heart started up a gymnastics routine in his ribcage, and he had to clench his teeth slightly.

Christ, calm down. Remember, he did try to maul you the other night. This could be a trap.

But if Elias was trying to trick them, well, surely there was little harm in letting Elias think it was working, at least for just a little longer.

"Snob."

"Hey, London may be a shithole, but it's my shithole."

"So you grew up here?"

Elias nodded. "Certainly did."

"Well, then, any recommendations on what a London virgin should see? Since you're the expert here."

"I mean, all the touristy stuff is back toward the city center, but it is worth seeing, I suppose, especially if you've never been to London. Buckingham Palace is grand. Westminster Abbey's very historical. Oh, and the Tower of London is always good. You might even see a ghost there."

"Well, what if I don't want to see a ghost?" Rowan asked. "What if I'm looking for something ... *else*?"

Elias frowned. "Like what?"

"Oh, I don't know..." Rowan poured himself a shot. Held Elias's gaze as he downed it, waiting for the spark of recognition in Elias's eyes. Surely, he knew by now that Rowan was on to him.

But he only looked confused. Rowan sighed, setting the empty shot glass down and leaning in, letting Elias's scent curl over him.

"Like a werewolf?"

Elias's face went white.

"How's your ribcage doing?"

"*You...*" Elias breathed.

"Yeah, me. I'd have thought you would have smelled me out by now. Or maybe ripped my face off, since you didn't get it done last night—"

Elias clapped a hand over Rowan's mouth, eyes darting over to the group of guys down at the other end of the bar. They were singing along to "Hey Jude" now, too loud to possibly hear the conversation Rowan and Elias were having. The hand covering Rowan's mouth was shaking.

After a moment, Elias slid off the bar stool, grabbing his book and tucking it under his left arm. The hand clamped over Rowan's mouth moved to grab a fistful of his jacket.

"Not here. Come with me."

He half-led, half-dragged Rowan toward the front door, then out onto the street. A few people passing gave them odd looks, so Rowan pulled himself out of Elias's grip, straightening his denim jacket with a yank and a sharp scowl at Elias.

"Mind telling me where the bloody hell we're going? I'm not a child, I don't need to be dragged about."

"My place. We can talk there."

And like that, he was off again, setting a brisk pace. Rowan matched it easily. He wanted answers as much as Elias wanted to get out of the public.

Elias led him into a dingy but decent building, then up two flights of stairs to an apartment door with chipped white paint. Elias fished out his keys, hands shaking and fingers fumbling, and finally unlocked the door, ushering Rowan inside, flipping on a lamp near the door. They were in the living room, which had a threadbare couch, a boxy television set, a wall of packed-full bookshelves, and a coffee table with an overflowing ashtray and a stack of books on it. The kitchen was tucked around the corner, and a hallway off the living room presumably led to Elias's bedroom and the bathroom. Elias deposited his book on top of the pile on the coffee table, then fished a pack of cigarettes from his pocket, placing one between his lips. Rowan took a seat on the couch, watching warily as the other man lit the cigarette with shaking fingers, hoping that he wouldn't accidentally set the place on fire by dropping the lighter into the shag carpet.

"So what gives?" Rowan asked as Elias took a drag. "You nearly tore off my face last night, and now you're sharing whiskey with me at a bar like nothing happened?"

Elias sighed out a cloud of smoke. "I didn't realize it was you."

"How? I smelled you out halfway across the bar!"

Elias opened his mouth to answer, but Rowan cut him off. "How'd you even get away? You're the one who left a trail of blood into the forest! I thought you...I thought they might have...you know..."

"Your concern is touching," Elias said. "There was a felled tree that had landed over a ditch. I hid under the tree until I was sure the cop chasing me was gone. He must have figured that the blood came from the dead deer."

"I hope you enjoyed that deer," Rowan ground out.

"Look, I'm sorry about what happened the other night—"

"Sorry? I didn't even want to start a fight! Did you not see me trying to move along without a fuss?"

"I've lived long enough to know not to trust what people say. For all I knew, you'd attack me as soon as my back was turned."

"Why would I do that?"

Elias raised an eyebrow. "You saw me. I'm smaller, I travel alone. I'm an easy target."

Rowan opened his mouth to respond, to argue, but then closed it. Elias did have a good point—he was an easy target. And he couldn't exactly blame the man for being suspicious or distrustful. He'd only been a werewolf for thirty years, but he had learned early that trust was something he had to give carefully and sparingly. And Elias...well, Elias may well have been decades older than him. Maybe even centuries.

"How old are you?" he asked.

Elias frowned. "Pardon?"

"How old are you?"

"Old."

"How old?"

"Why does it matter?" Elias asked, taking another drag from his cigarette.

"Just...wanted to know." Rowan dragged the white rubber toe of his Chuck Taylors along the carpet. "The prick who turned me was completely useless, and the last time I saw him, I told him I would tear his throat out with my teeth if I ever saw him again. Of course, it would be my rotten luck that he's the only werewolf I've met in the last three decades."

Elias's eyebrows climbed toward his hairline in surprise. Rowan smirked.

"Until now."

"Really?" Elias's brows furrowed.

"Swear on my mum."

"*I'm* the first werewolf you've met in thirty years?"

"On either side of the Iron Curtain."

Elias's expression turned sour. "What a disappointment this must be for you."

A twinge of pain went through Rowan, as real as if he'd been punched. He understood self-loathing, he'd had his share of bad days in the last three decades. But Elias's response, his clear disgust in himself, was like watching someone kick a puppy. Rowan frowned, shaking his head.

"I don't think you're a disappointment," he said. "Why would I think you're a disappointment?"

"I couldn't even sniff you out in a half-empty bar. You said it yourself."

"Eh. That's...that's whatever. You're not a disappointment."

"Look, I've been alive for over three hundred years, and this is all I have to show for it." Elias gestured around the living room. "If this is disappointment, then I don't know what it is."

If it were possible, Rowan's jaw would have hit the ground. "*Three hundred years?*"

"Yes. I was born during the English Civil War," Elias said. "I made it through Cromwell, the Great Plague, and the Great Fire unscathed, and I was starting to think I was one pretty lucky son of a bitch. Or, at least, I did until some mad werewolf decided to use me as a chew toy. I've been shuffling around this mortal coil for three hundred and twenty-nine years, and what you see is all I have to show for it."

"I don't think that's disappointing," Rowan said. "I... think that's amazing."

"Amazing?" Elias shook his head. "I don't think so."

"Why not?"

"It's not important." Elias flopped onto the couch, stubbing his cigarette out in the ashtray. He put another between his lips, but didn't light it. "What do you want from me?"

"I guess..." Rowan blew out a sigh, shoving his hair back from his forehead. "I guess I want to talk to you. You're the first person in thirty years that I can tell the truth to. The whole dirty, ugly truth."

Elias didn't respond for a moment, choosing instead to light another cigarette and taking a long drag. He breathed out, the smoke wreathing his head like a halo. Finally, he pinched his cigarette between his index and middle fingers, taking it out of his mouth and holding it there, smoke curling toward the ceiling.

"Why?"

"Why what?"

"Why do you want to trust me so much? You barely know me from Adam. I tried to tear your face off the other night."

"Well, I'm not holding that against you," Rowan chuckled. "To be honest, I probably would have done the same thing."

Elias didn't laugh. "You seem willing to put a lot of trust into someone you just met."

"Well," Rowan said. "Maybe I...want to get to know you a little better."

Elias snorted. "I'm not very good at making friends. Just want to warn you about that right now."

"Who said I just wanted to be friends?"

Elias went very still. A knot formed in Rowan's gut.

He'd lied about so many things for three decades, but there was one thing he'd lied about for longer than that, the first thing he'd ever lied about. He'd known from his teenage years that he'd fancied gents just as much as ladies. His first kiss had been a quick and dangerous thing, a stolen moment behind his school when he was in sixth form with a boy from his choir class named Chester. Rowan had wondered for months afterwards if Chester had felt the jolt of electricity that he had felt, if his heart had beat faster and his blood had sang in his veins. They never repeated the incident. Homosexuality wasn't just a sin, it was illegal, and would have likely resulted in jail time for both of them if they'd been caught.

It had been different on the continent. Some places, like Denmark and Poland, had decriminalized homosexuality a decade before Rowan made it over their borders. Others hadn't done it until the early sixties, with West Germany waiting until it was nearly 1970 to do so. Rowan had hardly had trouble finding an attractive person of either gender to pass a night with, and he'd always been careful for the sake of his partners, especially his male partners. They were, after all, the ones who faced the potential consequences. After all, he was nobody. A ghost story. He put down no roots, never gave out his true name. For all intents and purposes, Rowan Walsh stopped existing in 1941.

"What else would you want to be?" Elias asked, voice soft.

Rowan scooted a little closer. Elias's cigarette had burned down to ash, and Rowan took it, stubbing it out in the nasty ashtray. Elias watched his every move, wary, like the deer they'd both chased in the park. Rowan licked his lips, then leaned in, pressing them to Elias's.

Elias went stiff, and Rowan's gut sank. He'd been too caught up in his own feelings that it hadn't occurred to him that Elias was likely heterosexual—and even if he wasn't, he might not have been interested in Rowan. He broke away, feeling, for once, at a complete and total loss.

"I'm sorry, I'm sorry, I don't...I didn't think to...I should have asked—"

Elias took Rowan's face in his hands and swallowed his fumbling apologies with a kiss.

It was like coming home after being away for years. There was something comfortingly familiar about the feel of Elias's lips on his, as though they'd known each other for two lifetimes, not two days. Rowan looped his arms around Elias's neck, fingers twining into the curls at his nape. Relief rushed through him at the fact that Elias hadn't thrown a punch at him, but that relief turned to searing want when Elias caught Rowan's bottom lip between his teeth and gave a gentle tug. He gently pulled on Elias's hair, shivering at the soft moan he got in response.

Finally, they broke apart, panting slightly. In the low light of Elias's apartment, Rowan could see a faint blush across his cheeks, which, combined with the endorphins rushing through his blood, made him laugh, albeit a bit shakily.

"You know, I thought for a moment that you were going to beat the ever-loving shit out of me."

"That would have been rude of me."

"So...you..?"

Elias nodded. "I do, but, um...I like women, too. I know that might be a problem."

"Not for me." Rowan grinned. "You and I have similar tastes."

Hope bloomed in Elias's expression. "So you're..?"

"Bisexual as they come, mate. You're a talented kisser, by the way."

"Really? You're my first...anything in a few years."

"You're joking."

Elias shook his head.

"How? You're gorgeous."

And he meant it. Elias may have looked a little shaggy from first glance, and his fashion sense wasn't exactly the most stylish, but he really was gorgeous. The light from the lamp in the corner brought a shine to his hair, and the dampness outside had made it curl charmingly at the ends. Thick, dark eyelashes brushed against his cheekbones with every blink. And his eyes were downright enchanting.

He ducked his head at Rowan's words. "Oh, no, I'm...I'm really not..."

"Yes, you are, and I damn well meant what I said."

Elias flushed a little more. "And you...you really want to get to know me better?"

For the past three decades, Rowan's relationships had been strictly casual, never anything with the promise of long-term commitment. But something was different about Elias. He wasn't sure if it was because Elias was a werewolf, or bisexual, or even just because he had such a damn nice smile. But Rowan smiled, leaning in to press a gentle kiss—a promise—to Elias's lips.

"I damn well meant that, too."

***

"Ready for a busy night?"

Rowan was going to Epping Forest again.

It had been a month since his first and eventful trip, and the moon hung full and bright in the sky again. But this time, Rowan wasn't going alone. Across from him, Elias looked up from his book to give Rowan one of his barely there smiles. They were both dressed in jogging suits, this time of a slightly better quality than the old, ratty thing Rowan had been wearing last month. He'd never been so happy to throw something away.

He'd never been quite so happy, period. Life had definitely taken a turn for the better since the night he'd met Elias. He'd gotten a job in a warehouse down by the Thames, had moved in with Elias and out of that nasty hotel he'd been living in. He and Elias had made the decision to commit to a relationship. He had made a decision to stop being a ghost story and start being himself again. It was a new decade, a new Britain, and the world was his and Elias's for the taking.

It wasn't perfect. Neither of them made much money. Elias's landlord had threatened to throw them out if they were going to share his apartment, so they'd had to move into a flat with two bedrooms instead, which took more money out of their already-limited budget. Rowan's job was mind-numbing menial labor that left him sore and tired when he got home. They both still woke screaming from nightmares in the middle of the night. And Elias preferred to drown his problems in whiskey and cigarettes than address them, leaving Rowan in the dark about his early years even though they clearly troubled him.

But even with all of that, climbing into bed next to Elias at the end of the day, snuggling close, pressing his chest into Elias's warm back, was worth it.

"Hopefully, not as eventful as last time," Elias said. "I don't need quite that much adventure."

"Oh, but where's the fun in that?"

The train rumbled into Loughton, and they both stood, heading for the doors. The air was warm and held the promise of summer. Even the skies were clear. Elias tilted his face skyward.

"I think it's going to be a good night."

"I think so, too." Rowan slid behind Elias, slipping his arms around his waist. "And when we get home, we can make it a *great* night."

Elias chuckled. "As long as we don't miss the train."

"You're never going to let me live that down, are you?"

"You could have taken a taxi, you know. You're the one who was daft enough to walk back to Tower Hamlets in the middle of the night."

"At least I didn't spend the night sleeping on the forest floor."

"Still safer than walking back home in the middle of the night. I am, after all, the biggest and meanest thing in the forest."

"Walking twenty kilometers in the middle of the night still isn't the stupidest thing I've done."

"Oh?" Elias glanced over his shoulder. "Care to share?"

"Only if you're planning on sharing some of yours."

"Git."

"You love it."

Elias turned in his arms, the two of them now pressed chest-to-chest on the empty platform. Rowan's heart skipped a beat, just like it did every time he looked into those gorgeous blue-gray eyes. He smiled.

"Give us a kiss?"

"In public? You're bold tonight."

His grin turned wolfish. "Must be a full moon."

Elias leaned in, and Rowan puckered his lips in anticipation. But Elias bypassed them completely, whispering into his ear.

"Last one to the park has to shower second."

He broke away and ran for the station, leaving Rowan gobsmacked and reeling. He shook his head, Elias's words registering, and scowled.

"Hey, no fair! I'm not showering second! You always use up all the hot water!"

"Well then, you should start running!"

"I don't even get a kiss for good luck?"

Elias's didn't respond. He was already down the stairs, out of the station, and running down the sidewalk toward Epping Forest. Rowan shook his head, unable to stop the smile growing on his face, and hurried after Elias, ready for whatever the night had in store.

LUCIFER'S LIGHTS

Karen Garvin

The sweet vanilla scent of cut summer grass
wafts up from beneath our bare feet,
the sharp blades pricking our soles.

We take in the flavor of the night,
savoring the humidity of the languid air,
and give chase to little sparks of light
that twinkle like stars in the summer sky.

We race about the yard in darkness,
anticipating the first flicker of life
from the street light in front of the house.

Jars are readied for their new tenants,
their lids punctured by holes
so the fireflies can inhale.

By bedtime, the glass jars are filled
with scintillating insects,
each one flickering
on-off, on-off, on-off
in syncopated rhythm
to some unheard song.

We worship their beauty,
their pulsing bewitches us,
speaks to us
of untold stories
of childhood eternal.

Enraptured,
we open the jars,
set them free.

I'm Jessie Rhodes, and that's my poem, one that I wrote several years ago during my freshman English literature class. I was convinced at the time that poetry was going to become my road to riches, but this poem turned out to be the only thing I wrote all semester that I actually liked. Maybe that had more to do with the assignments that the professor handed out, but in any case, I *still* like this poem. I called it "Fireflies Inhaling," but I'm not sure if the title fits anymore.

What I did learn about myself that first year of college was that poetry wasn't my strong suit, and I didn't really belong in English lit. I belonged in science. My childhood love of fireflies came through in this brief poem, and it showed me my own true path. That's how I ended up studying entomology and becoming a researcher who studies fireflies and the fascinating enzyme that makes them glow.

* * *

"How can the results be so different from group to group?" I asked, glancing over at my lab partner.

Gary shrugged and toyed with a mechanical pencil, turning it over and over in his hands. He only fiddled with things when he was really agitated, and I gathered from the speed of the twirls that he must be pretty upset right now. Unfortunately, since I'm the head of this research project, I have to ask the kind of difficult questions that will probably only make him angrier — and give me an upset stomach. I swallowed my angst; no sense postponing the inevitable.

"Gary, are you sure about these results?" I knew that he was careful about recording data, but the numbers made no sense at all. I had to eliminate the possibility of human error.

"I double-checked everything," said Gary. He pressed his lips together and gave me a dark look, knitting his brows together. "The equipment records the numbers, too. If you don't believe my paperwork, then check the calibration on the scanners."

"It's not that I don't believe you," I said, perhaps a mite too quickly. "And we just calibrated the equipment last week. It doesn't go off that quickly. But you have to admit that the test results don't make sense."

"We can't be sure that we are interpreting them correctly."

"What do you mean?" I put the clipboard down and sat forward. The plastic chair creaked under my weight and I could feel the edge of the seat buckle.

Gary put the pencil down and rubbed his face. "Look, we're treating all the fireflies as though they are the same, right?"

I nodded. "Sure. They are all the same species, *Photinus pyralis*."

"Okay, but this group," he waved at the floor-to-ceiling wall of glass, behind which were rows of small terrariums filled with insects, "they're all wild-caught, not bred here in the lab." Gary paused and folded his arms.

"And?" I prompted, when it was clear that he was waiting for me to fill in the blanks. But I had no idea where he was going with his argument.

"Well, we have no idea of exactly where each insect was caught. They might all be members of the same species, but we need to be able to account for individual variations and for any adaptations that groups have made to their local area."

"Of course." I nodded slowly, taking in the idea. "But where do we even start?"

The problem was that our providers deliver the insects and only concern themselves with providing live, healthy specimens for our research. But they make no attempt to tag the insects in the field; fireflies aren't exactly elephants or rhinos and it's pretty difficult to mark each one out in the field without it either escaping or getting damaged by an overzealous insect hunter with a heavy hand on the paint brush. So up until now there had been little reason to record exactly where each insect was captured; besides, they flew, and who knew how far the little things ranged each night?

I picked up the clipboard again and scanned the numbers. "All right. Let's run the experiment again next week and see if we get different results." I glanced up at the clock.

"Hey, it's almost quitting time, and it's Friday. Let's clean up the lab and worry about this puzzle next week."

I could see that Gary wasn't too pleased with my eagerness to be rid of the problem, but that's how I am. I love my work, really! But sometimes I just have to chuck it aside in favor of doing something else. I'm convinced that my brain works better that way, that my unconscious is somehow busily chugging away at coming up with a solution even while my conscious mind is engaged in watching a movie. Or playing a video game.

"Come on, Gary," I said. "Take a break from it and we'll come back on Monday with a fresh outlook on the whole thing. And a whole new week to collect more data. Don't you want that?"

Glumly, he began sorting papers and tucking them away into manila folders. He still had the aura of someone who was in high dudgeon.

Whatevs. I snatched up my backpack and shrugged into my coat, heading toward the door before my partner — my *junior* lab partner—could talk me into working late on a Friday night.

* * *

An incessant ringing woke me up, each loud buzz a jab to my eardrums. I made a mental note to change my ringtone and got out of bed, hurling the blanket aside in my frustration. It had better not be some stupid telemarketer calling me on a Saturday morning.

I looked at the phone before answering it and saw that the caller was Gary. He'd only ever called me on my cell once before and my stomach clenched as I dragged my thumb across the screen.

"Hey, what's up, Gary?" My voice was creaky with sleep, and I had to clear my throat and repeat the question.

"Jessie, you need to get down to the lab right away. We have a situation here."

"What? What do you mean 'a situation'?" I stared at my bed, wishing I could just crawl back under the fluffy white duvet.

"I can't tell you on the phone, it's not secure. Just get here as soon as you can."

And then he hung up on me. For a moment I stared at my phone. I had no idea what to think. Our research work wasn't hazardous and it was really unlikely that rival scientists were trying to steal our manuscripts. Gary had sounded concerned and he wasn't one for practical jokes. It occurred to me that I hadn't asked him if he was okay, and I felt a slight twinge of guilt, but I pushed it aside.

I dressed in a hurry, climbing into jeans and a sweater, and headed out. I didn't even wait for the car to warm up before I swung away from the curb and wended my way out onto the main road. The lab was at least twenty minutes away, but it was an easy drive and on a Saturday morning, the traffic would be light.

But then my stomach rumbled with the vigor it reserved for early morning and I decided the "situation" could wait another minute or two. I saw no good reason to face a problem on an empty stomach and I had no idea how long I'd be tied up at the lab. Besides, Gary would have the sense to phone the authorities if there was a real emergency and once I got my food I could take the freeway to make up for the lost time.

I drove to the local coffee shop. Fortunately, the store

wasn't crowded and I was back in the car with my coffee and bagel within a couple of minutes. The phone rang again, and I put it on speakerphone.

"How far away are you?" Gary's voice was breathy and indistinct.

"A few miles, I'm driving as fast as I can."

"Are you almost here? I called you twenty-five minutes ago."

"You're timing me?" I snapped. "Gary, I had to get dressed. I don't sleep in my clothing." *There.* Let him wonder what I meant by that. I tossed the bagel back in the paper bag and secured the coffee in the cup holder.

"What's that noise?"

"Road noise," I lied.

"Well, come in the back door when you arrive. I think they're trying to get out the front."

"Who? The fireflies?" *Geez, just close the damn lab door!*

"Just hurry." Gary hung up again. I was aggravated that he ignored my question, but his abrupt behavior was also worrisome. It wasn't like him to act like this. Concerned that all of our fireflies and all of our research work was about to go up in a figurative (I hoped) puff of smoke, I peeled out of the parking lot and caught the tire on the curb just enough to make the coffee slosh out of the cup and spill onto the passenger side mat. I shouted a few adult words and by the time I reached the lab my hands were slick with perspiration.

Only two cars were in the front parking lot. I recognized Gary's truck with its heavily tinted windows and a fatigued-looking white sedan that belonged to a researcher in the lab next to ours. I drove around to the back of the building and parked next to the loading dock.

I eyed the coffee puddle and plucked some napkins from the glove box and threw them on the floor, then I opened the bag and took two bites of the bagel before putting it away. As I climbed out of the car my anxiety level rose.

I wished Gary had been more forthcoming with answers. I didn't know what I was getting myself into, so I let myself into the small foyer as noiselessly as I could and peeked around the corner before entering the service corridor that ran the length of the building. Nothing seemed out of the ordinary, but the sensation of being watched was overwhelming.

I risked a glance over my shoulder, certain that someone would be walking behind me, but no one was there. But instead of feeling relieved, cold chills ran up my spine. I quickened my pace. Our lab was midway along the building and it seemed to take forever to reach it.

I slid my access card through the card reader and eased the lab door open a few inches. When nothing jumped out I opened it wider and stepped into the lab's back room. Everything seemed normal, except only half of the ceiling lights were working. I made a mental note to put in a repair request and checked the corridor again. Still empty.

I shut the door and let my eyes adjust to the dim lighting. There was a sudden movement in the right corner and I jumped back when Gary stood up from where he had been crouching.

Another string of adult words flew out of my mouth before I could stop myself. I didn't like to swear at work; it wasn't professional, and it just encouraged others to be crude. But sometimes adult words were needed. Like now. I clutched my coat. "Gary, you almost gave me a heart attack! What's wrong? Are you hurt?"

"Shhh. Keep your voice down. They don't know I'm still here."

"Who?"

He gestured for me to squat down and I crossed the room in a semi-crouch, avoiding the windows and the door leading to the main lab. Even in the half-light Gary looked pale. Well, Gary was *always* pale because he was an albino, but still. He looked ghastly.

But all my stupid ghost puns died on my lips when I looked into Gary's eyes. I saw his fear, felt his fear, tasted his fear. I swallowed convulsively as panic surged through my body and I had to fight to keep my emotions under control.

"Gary, please tell me what is happening."

Gary waved his hand to indicate that we should hide. I thought it was ridiculous to crawl under the lab table, but I can't lie: I also felt better after we were concealed. People who say fear isn't contagious don't know what the hell they're talking about.

"Make sure your phone's ringer is off," Gary whispered.

I stared at him.

"Do it!" he hissed.

Swallowing again, I pulled out my phone and silenced it. "There. Satisfied?"

Gary nodded.

"So, what is going on?" I peered out from under the table, looking for any stray legs that would indicate intruders.

"They've gotten out of containment."

My eyebrows shot up. "This is about the fireflies? That's all?"

Our project is to study luciferase, which is the enzyme that fireflies and other bioluminescent creatures use to produce light. The main goal of the research is to find ways to use the enzyme in cancer detection, and up until this last test we had used synthetic luciferase out of concern for the native firefly populations. However, the manmade enzyme had some quirks that defied our expectations, and our lab supervisor had suggested changing over to studying natural enzymes. Hence, part of our science lab has become an insect zoo, where we have established a selective breeding program to create fireflies that can produce more luciferase than their wild cousins. And it's complete with a live webcam for the entertainment of insomniacs worldwide.

I thought about the fireflies we had in our terrariums. There were thousands of them, and rounding them up was going to be a huge chore, not to mention that there was no way of tracking our test results—even if the results made no sense. We'd be forced to start over, even if we hadn't decided earlier that we were going to. On the one hand, I was sick at the loss of all that work, but it gave us a good reason to rerun the experiment and might avoid any awkward inquiries into our data collection methods.

"No, it's not all. It's just the beginning."

I was so absorbed in my thoughts that I missed what Gary said. "Well, we need to get them *re*contained. We can sort them out later." *Maybe.* It's not like we had marked all of them. In the first few terrariums we'd filled we had painstakingly painted blue or white dots on the fireflies, but it was tedious and time-consuming, so we had stopped. It was far easier to mark each terrarium and it worked for our record-keeping, but now? Ugh!

I began crawling out from under the table to assess the damage when Gary caught hold of my elbow. I winced as his thin fingers dug into my flesh.

"Didn't you hear me? Don't go out there."

Irritated, I pulled my arm away, but Gary flung out his other arm to prevent me from moving forward. "Just listen."

"All right." I sat cross-legged on the cold floor and wished I had not lost my coffee.

"I left my coat in the lab last night," said Gary. "I had a date, so I stopped by to fetch my coat on the way to the movie."

Gary had a date? What other surprise would he throw my way? I tried not to overreact to this unusual admission of personal information, and I must have succeeded in maintaining a poker face because he didn't comment on my reaction.

"All the fireflies were out of the terrariums, but they weren't just anywhere. They were lined up on the counter-top. They were in *formation*!"

"That could've been a coincidence," I said, as much to reassure Gary as myself. Fireflies were, well, insects. "They're not exactly Einsteins. And how did they get out of the glass enclosure, anyway?"

"I don't know how they got out, and I didn't see any damage to the terrariums," said Gary. "But they were organized. You can check the surveillance videos yourself if you don't believe me."

I didn't doubt Gary's powers of observation. He was as cool as they came. Perhaps I was upset because I just wasn't used to Gary getting emotional about anything.

"Well, we can't hide under the table all day. And it's not like they sting."

"No," admitted Gary. "But wait. You've got to see this."

He pulled his phone out of his pocket and brought up a video. It showed the fireflies arranged in five clumps of three parallel lines on the black countertop. The left row of insects in the first group blinked once, then the second row of fireflies blinked twice, and then the third row blinked three times. There was a short pause and the message swept across the countertop from group to group in a slow rhythm.

"What the hell?" My mouth fell open. Yes, I knew fireflies signaled to one another, but not like this. Not en masse.

"Keep watching," said Gary. There was an undercurrent of excitement in his voice edging out the fear. The scientist in him was trying to reassert itself.

Once the last row had finished blinking, all of the insects began flashing. The pattern seemed familiar: three short blinks, three long blinks, three short blinks. Over and over and over.

"Do you see it?"

"Uhm, I'm not sure." In my gut I *knew* what it was, but I didn't want to admit it. Somehow giving voice to what I was trying *not* to think would make it more real. Or surreal.

"It's Morse Code," declared Gary, in his best don't-argue-with-me voice.

I shook my head. "It ... it can't be. That's got to be a coincidence."

"Is it?" Gary scooted closer to me so that our faces were only a couple of inches apart. "Do you really believe that? Can you watch this video and tell me you don't see intelligence at work?"

He had me. No, I couldn't deny what I had seen in the video, but how could I credit the fireflies with that kind of knowledge? "How would they know Morse Code?"

"I don't know. But Jessie, it gets even more bizarre—the fireflies are positioned on the counter exactly where our live webcam can pick them up the best."

I cocked my head. "What are you saying?"

"This message is 'SOS.' And it's going out over the internet. The whole world can see it."

"*If* anyone is watching our webcam," I snorted. "I'm sure our audience of twelve could rally a world army."

Gary's mouth turned down at the corners. "Funny you should say that."

"What?"

"World army."

This time I could not hold back the laughter. Whether it was really funny or whether the adrenaline had just worn off, I don't know. But for several minutes I couldn't stop laughing and Gary's dark scowl only made the situation more hilarious. Finally I wiped my eyes.

"Gary," I gasped, still out of breath, "All we have to do is disconnect the webcam."

"Yes, but the connection is in the main lab."

"Are you afraid to go in there?" I indicated the other room with a nod. "They're not dangerous, so really, why are we hiding under this table?"

"They *weren't* dangerous," mumbled Gary. But he crawled out from under the table and offered me his hand, which I accepted with all the grace I could muster.

"All right, let's both go and assess the damage," I said. As senior researcher it was my call, anyway. I wondered if Gary had expected me to brave the fireflies on my own. I pulled open the door to the main lab before either of us could have second thoughts.

The fireflies were still lined up in formation on the counter, just as they had been in Gary's video. They were quiescent now, and none moved so much as an antenna as I approached the table with slow, cautious steps. For a moment I wondered if they were dead. But when I was within two feet of the counter every firefly began blinking.

Blink. Blink. Blink.

They flashed in perfect unison, hundreds of little yellow-green strobe lights. I've always loved fireflies and this caught me off guard, taking me back to my earliest childhood memories. I stopped my advance and backed up. The fireflies went dark.

"This is *not* normal," said Gary, his voice rising half an octave. He took a step toward the back room.

"Can you disconnect the webcam?" I needed Gary to focus on the camera so I could think of a way to get the fireflies back into containment, preferably without killing them.

"Yes. Okay."

Gary inched along the wall, keeping as much space as possible between himself and the fireflies. I have never seen him this nervous. When he reached the corner where the computer was plugged in, he began yanking out cords.

Immediately every insect took to the air. They swarmed Gary. He screwed his eyes shut and screamed, swatting wildly as the fireflies landed on his face and began crawling into his nose and ears. Gary tried to close his mouth, but the fireflies had already found this human cavern and were filling his mouth.

I was stunned. I couldn't move for what seemed like an eternity—and it probably was for Gary. I rushed to his side and began sweeping handfuls of the fireflies away from his head. It was a waste of time. Just as I brushed some away, more filled the space. Gary's face disappeared under a mass of seething fireflies. He began to choke.

I panicked and began thumping Gary on the back. He coughed hard several times and retched. With one hand Gary managed to pull his shirt up over the lower part of his face while he pinched his nose shut with the other hand.

I heard a muttered thanks through the ball of bugs as I steered Gary toward the back room. I didn't know if we would be any safer there, but I had to do something. None of the insects were on me; it was as though I repelled them somehow. Or maybe they were angry at Gary for cutting off the camera.

As we moved through the door separating the front part of the lab from the back, we passed the small cleaning closet. I let go of Gary and pulled out the vacuum cleaner. It was one of those bagless models with a transparent container. I plugged it in and powered it up, aiming the suction hose at Gary's head.

The fireflies tumbled over one another in the stream of air as the vacuum sucked them in. I swept the hose over Gary's face, careful not to jab him in the eye, and I didn't turn off the machine until I was sure every one of the insects was contained. It bothered me to think I might have just killed most of our specimens, but it needed to be done. I switched off the vacuum and turned my attention to my lab partner.

Gary was a mess. Few people realize that lighting bugs can bite, even though they normally don't. He had little red spots all over his face and it looked swollen.

"Gary, did you swallow any of them?"

He nodded grimly. I pulled my phone from my pocket and dialed 911. I didn't know how toxic they were to humans, but he might have been poisoned by the lucibufagin they produce, which is a defensive chemical that makes them unappealing to eat. Lizards and even small animals were known to sicken and die after eating fireflies, so I wasn't going to take any chances. I asked for an ambulance and poison control. Then I walked Gary out the back door and we sat in my car to wait for the EMTs.

"What do you think will happen now?" Gary's voice was strained from shouting and coughing.

"Well, there's a lot of clean-up," I said, thinking about the insects in the vacuum cleaner. "After we've gotten you taken care of, I'll go back to the lab and try to get the fireflies sorted out. I have no idea of how many are destroyed." My thoughts were glum, not only because my research was gone, but my employment prospects might also be on the line. And Gary's, too.

"Destroyed? Kill them all," rasped Gary. "Kill every damn one of them."

I was surprised at the steel in his voice, but I probably shouldn't have been. I looked at Gary, sitting rigidly in my passenger seat, and I saw the rage in his eyes. And then movement caught my eye and I turned my head to watch the ambulance as it rolled up to the building.

When I greeted the medics I said Gary had accidentally swallowed some fireflies when they escaped from containment. I left out the part of the story about Morse Code; no reason to make them think we needed psychiatric help.

Gary sat in the ambulance while the medics took his blood pressure and examined the welts on his face. He gave me a thumbs-up, and I smiled and unclenched my hands, willing myself to relax. I hadn't realized until now just how tense I was. Remembering my breakfast, I headed over to my car. And that was when I heard the noise.

It was a ping, as though something was hitting the building's steel-plated back door, only it sounded more like *many* somethings hitting and bouncing off the metal. I shivered.

There was a rectangular window in the door with reinforced glass, but it had been painted over some time ago. I didn't want to go back in the building, but I needed to know what was making that noise. I took out my car key and began scraping off the ugly green latex. After I'd cleared off several inches of paint all I could see was blackness punctuated by rhythmic yellow flashes. It was the fireflies from the lab, jammed up against the window. They had not only survived the vacuum cleaner—they'd gotten out of that, too.

It was a relief to know I hadn't killed them, but now how would I get them back into containment? I'd have to go around to the front door and let the building engineer know to keep the back door locked.

I returned to the ambulance to tell Gary about this latest development. The morning sun had just topped the trees ringing the parking lot and I glanced at the sky. I saw a large dark cloud and thought that for once the weather report had been accurate.

But it was too low to be a rain cloud, and as I stared at it the mass seemed to expand and collapse upon itself like an accordion. Then it grew darker and darker until it was jet-black. Streaks of yellow shot through it, but it was not like lightning.

No, it was not like lightning at all.

"Get inside!" I rushed toward the ambulance, gesturing

toward the sky. One of the medics was standing by the back door of the vehicle talking to the other man, who was inside the truck with Gary. He half-turned in my direction. "Get inside!" I repeated, waving my arms. He probably thought I was off my rocker, but then he looked up and saw the black cloud and let out a low whistle.

"Storm comin' Charlie! Looks like a bad one, too. We'd better finish up here."

At that moment Gary poked his head out of the ambulance. "Jessie?"

"Are they releasing you, Gary?" I asked. I didn't know if I wanted them to haul him away to the hospital or if I'd rather he was here with me. Or whether it would be better if I went to the hospital along with him. I didn't relish the idea of being here by myself with that cloud coming our way. And even Gary's company would only make it two humans to millions of insects. We needed to tell others about the fireflies, but who would listen?

I crossed my arms, hugging myself. I felt cold despite the warm jacket I was still wearing.

"He should probably go to the emergency room for observation," cautioned the medic who was not-Charlie.

"Can I go with him? In the ambulance?"

The technician looked me over. "You his girlfriend or something?"

"Or something. We work together. He was injured in the workplace and I'm his supervisor so I should keep an eye on him." I shot Gary a look that said *yes, I know I'm not your supervisor, but don't argue with me now.*

The medic appeared to hesitate, but then shrugged his shoulders. "You can ride in the back if you want, but it's not a comfortable ride. You'd be better to take your own car, if you have one."

I didn't tell him that I was afraid to drive with that "storm" coming, and in truth, I wasn't sure if that was the reason I didn't want to take my car. I felt an odd sense of foreboding that told me that Gary and I shouldn't part company right now. So without another word, I pushed my way up into the ambulance.

Charlie was belting Gary in for the ride as the second technician closed the back of the ambulance. I felt a sense of relief rush through me with the doors closed and sat next to Gary, sagging against the wall. Charlie started the engine and soon the ambulance was pulling out of the parking lot.

This particular ambulance didn't have rear windows, or side windows, so we had no idea of what was happening with the cloud. I leaned forward to peer through the opening to the front of the ambulance and looked out the windshield. I could see nothing except the road and regular traffic. The sky seemed darker than it had been, but that might have been an illusion.

We drove on in silence until the ambulance rolled up to the emergency room doors at the hospital. Charlie helped Gary climb out the back and I followed, feeling like a lost puppy dog. They escorted Gary up to the registration counter and pushed some papers toward the nurse behind the desk, then left us standing there by ourselves.

"You didn't get to ride in a wheelchair," I teased Gary.

Gary cut his eyes in my direction but didn't rise to the joke. The receptionist started asking him questions, and while he was busy with the paperwork, I looked around. The emergency room wasn't crowded, but an entire family that must have spanned at least four generations appeared to fill one end of it. Two snot-nosed little kids were sitting on the floor, picking at something on the carpet, their parents oblivious to the germ fest their children were ingesting. I wanted to say something and thought better of it; there was no telling how some folks would respond to a random stranger poking her nose into their business.

I turned back to Gary. He was digging in his pocket for his wallet, still immersed in the hospital's bureaucratic red tape. At least he was well enough to deal with it. After a few minutes more, the nurse indicated for us to take a seat and wait.

We chose two chairs on the opposite side of the waiting room from the Addams family. I pulled my jacket closed and sat down.

"What now?" asked Gary.

"I was about to ask you that. Do they want to keep you in the hospital? Because I might have to call our supervisor and let him know that you were injured in the lab. Well, I'll probably have to do that, anyway." I rubbed the back of my neck. I'd never had to deal with anything like this before.

"I think they just want to run more tests," said Gary. "The itching is starting to fade."

"You aren't poisoned, then?"

"I don't think so." Gary sighed. "Look, I don't really want to go back to the lab. They seem to have it in for me."

I bit my lip. What could I say? The fireflies *had* attacked him.

"Jess?"

"I know. I don't blame you for not wanting to go back. I guess I just don't want to have to face them by myself," I said.

"We work pretty well together as a team, huh?" said Gary. But his tone of voice made it clear that it wasn't a question.

"Yeah." I could feel my ears growing warm and hoped that Gary wasn't paying too much attention to the way that I looked. So, it was a relief that before he could say anything else awkward or maudlin, the nurse called him back to the counter and indicated for him to go to an exam room. Gary headed into the tiny room and disappeared from sight.

Today was getting weirder and weirder. I pushed out of the chair and went to the window, focusing my attention on the sky. It had gotten lighter again and the strange cloud seemed to have disappeared. I breathed out a long, ragged sigh, jammed my hands into my pockets, and went in search of a coffee vending machine.

* * *

"Jess. Jessie." Something touched me and in the strange dream I was inhabiting I felt paralyzed with fear. Another touch, but this time I jolted upright, my eyes flashing open. I took in the ugly fluorescent glare of the waiting room. Why were hospitals so damn ugly?

"Gary. Are you done? Is everything okay?"

"Yeah, I'm fine. I can leave. Are you okay?"

"Mmm, I fell asleep. I was having a weird dream." I got up and we walked toward the door, and then I remembered that we didn't have a ride. "Damn. I should have brought my car."

"Don't worry about it, I can spring for a taxi."

I rummaged in my purse for my wallet, but Gary shook his head and refused to take any money. We waited in companionable silence, but my angst returned as soon as the taxi arrived. We knew that we had to go back to the lab. I gave the taxi driver the address and sank back against the seat.

The taxi dropped us off at the front of the oh-so-normal building. We stood for a moment, then I squared my shoulders and marched up to the door and swiped my access card in the lock. For a moment I thought that it wouldn't open. I felt a rush of elation, thinking that we had a valid reason to leave, but then the green light came on and I heard the door click. Resolutely, I pulled it open and stepped inside, Gary following just behind.

We paused in the lobby. Nothing seemed amiss, so we headed to our office suite and went into the reception area. Unfortunately, none of the labs or other work spaces were visible from there, so we had no way of knowing what lay on the other side of the blond wood door that separated the reception area from the rest of our space.

"Ready?" I help up my access card, trying not to let my hand shake. The growing lump in my throat threatened to choke me.

Gary swallowed noisily and stared at the door.

"Why don't I go in first?" I suggested. Not that I wanted to, but knowing Gary would be out here in the reception area was reassuring. "I'll take a look at the lab and come back to report to you. I'll just be a couple of minutes. Okay?"

Gary nodded.

Before I could change my mind, I opened the wood door and entered the small area behind the reception room. Our lab actually consisted of three working spaces, plus a small kitchenette and bathrooms equipped with showers. Everything seemed normal, and I walked slowly down the hall and peered into each of the three labs. The first two were dark, although I could clearly see through the Plexiglas windows that the labs were unoccupied and looked undisturbed. And then I got to the third lab — ours — and it was anything but normal.

It, too, was dark, but it wasn't unoccupied. Every square inch of wall space inside the room appeared to be covered with fireflies, and the back door looked like it had been blown off its hinges, although there didn't seem to be any other damage to the room. I turned on my heel and ran back to the reception area.

"Well?" Gary's voice sounded strained, but I pretended not to hear his fear. I had enough of my own to deal with right now.

"Our lab is filled with fireflies," I said. "And the back door is open."

"We didn't leave it open, did we?"

"Nope. The door was shut when we left, although some of the fireflies had gotten out and were at the building's back door."

"Then how—" Gary rubbed his face.

"I'm going to call Patrick. I should have done it hours ago." I pulled out my phone and called our lab supervisor. To his credit, he answered on the third ring, even though it was now Saturday night. I started to explain about the fireflies but Patrick cut me off.

"They're all out of containment? How did you let that happen?"

"I didn't," I protested. "Gary found them out this morning."

"Why was he at the lab on Saturday morning?"

I tried to explain again, but Patrick was having trouble following my story. Finally, he agreed to meet us at the lab.

"Well?" prompted Gary.

"He's coming down to help us clean up the lab."

"Well, he doesn't know what he's in for."

"Gary, do I detect sarcasm?" Patrick wasn't the most helpful of supervisors, but he was a decent guy to work for. He just wasn't a hands-on sort of supervisor.

We waited, mostly impatiently, for our boss. My stomach growled but I refused to go back to the kitchen. The snack machine was a known source of stale crackers, and the way my throat felt I'd probably choke on them.

Patrick arrived forty minutes later. Once I'd explained the day's events to him, we took him back to the lab. Just as I'd done, he peered into each of the other labs, but when he reached ours he stopped dead.

"What the hell is this?"

"I told you," I said. "This isn't just our fireflies."

"I thought you said they'd gotten *out*, not that others had gotten *in*."

"We're not really sure what's happening," I said. "I was hoping maybe you'd seen similar behavior in other fireflies. Or in other species. Have you?" My words tumbled out in a rush, but I didn't care if Patrick thought I was scared. I *was* scared.

"This is not normal behavior of any insect species I've encountered," said Patrick. "You said they attacked Gary?"

"They swarmed me," said Gary. "All over my head. They tried to suffocate me, and they bit me all over my face."

Patrick finally seemed to notice the bumps all over Gary's face. I wondered if he'd thought Gary had an acne outbreak. I stifled the nervous giggle before it could leave my lips.

"All right, Jessie, what do you think? You said the fireflies didn't even land on you. Is it a male/female thing? Do you think I'll be safe if I go in there?" Patrick nodded toward the lab.

"I don't know." *How the hell would I know?* "I mean, I don't even know if fireflies recognize that there's a difference between male and female humans."

"I pulled their plug," said Gary.

"What?" Patrick gave him a look that said *you're an idiot.*

But Gary didn't waver under Patrick's glare. "I pulled out the cords to the webcam. The fireflies were broadcasting a message and I shut them down. Then they attacked me."

"Show him the video, Gary."

Gary pulled up the video and handed his phone to Patrick, who watched the short movie with ever-growing confusion.

"It's Morse Code. S-O-S," said Gary.

"I checked. He's right," I said, just in case Patrick wouldn't take Gary's word for it.

"I'll be damned." Patrick handed the phone back to Gary and turned his attention on the lab. "Well, we have to do something about this mess. The ruined research is one thing, but if we don't clear this out the building supervisor will be hell-bent on evicting us. I'm going in."

"Wait ..."

But Patrick opened the door and went into the lab. He moved slowly, stepping with exaggerated care, and turned on the lights. The walls were coated with insects, and every surface was covered with them. But none of them seemed to take notice of Patrick.

He moved around the room, taking stock of the situation, and then pulled out his own phone and began recording the scene. And that's when it started.

A group of fireflies on the lab table started blinking in unison. Were they spelling out some coded words? I knew only the S-O-S code so I had no way of knowing whether this was just blinking or communication.

Beside me, Gary had his own phone out and was recording the same scene. "We should write down the code," he said. "Do you have any paper?"

"What? No."

"Go and get some."

I nodded and went to the reception area to fetch stationery supplies. When I got back everything was much the same, although Gary was getting excited.

"I think it's a message, not just random flashing. Get ready to write this down."

Gary started dictating dots and dashes, and I tried as best I could to keep up with the dictation, but I've never been anyone's secretary and I soon fell behind and started getting frustrated. After a few minutes I handed the pencil and paper to Gary. "Here, why don't you try writing and I'll record the video? I can't write that fast."

We switched places and continued trying to track the "conversation" that the fireflies were having with us. Patrick came back into the hallway and none of the insects followed him. I felt some relief that they weren't showing any aggression and hoped that they'd stay that way.

"Okay, it seems to be repeating now," said Gary. "I'm going to go look this up. Want to help me decipher it?"

"Sure."

We left Patrick staring at the lab and went to the kitchenette. I made some coffee for myself and we started decoding the message, beginning with the common letters like "e" and "a" and working our way through the less-common letters. Eventually we deciphered the few minutes' worth of blinking. It *was* a message.

"What is this?" drawled Gary. "It's almost like English."

I stared at the paper for a moment, then with a jolt, I recognized it. "It *is* English, Gary! It's Middle English."

"I'm not familiar with that."

"Well, I was a literature major before I turned to science. I read Chaucer, and this is exactly the kind of language he used. The fireflies are speaking Middle English!"

Gary rubbed his brow. At that moment Patrick came into the kitchenette and gave me a pleading look. I knew that he was hoping I'd "magic" this problem away.

"Anything?" Patrick asked, glancing over his shoulder toward the lab.

"Jessie can read it," said Gary. He pushed the sheet of paper toward me.

"Well?" prompted our supervisor.

"Hold on, I'm a bit rusty..."

"You're *rusty*?" said Patrick. "You read science journals every day. What is this, remedial education?"

"She's translating, all right?" snapped Gary.

Patrick's mouth formed a perfect O. I tried not to laugh at his expression but it wasn't often that we managed to catch him so off guard.

"It's in Middle English," I explained. I reached for the pencil and began writing a modern translation of the fireflies' message.

Gary and Patrick edged closer to me as I wrote. I resisted the urge to cover the writing with my hand, as I'd done so often in third grade when my best friend tried to copy my work. I translated the last few words and picked up the paper. I cleared my throat and began to read.

"Greetings, children of Men. We are the Aelfdene, children of Wymond the Protector. We mean you no harm and beg you treat us likewise. We seek a boon and ask you to hear our request."

I put the paper down. "There must be more to the message."

Gary shook his head. "No, it just repeated."

"Sooooo ..." Patrick looked from me to Gary.

"We need to reply, obviously," said Gary. "Jess, can you compose a message, too?"

I bit my lip. Translating *from* a language was one thing, but writing in it was another skill—one that I wasn't sure I had. But I had to try. I was the only one who had any inkling of the language and I didn't think we had months for Gary and Patrick to learn Middle English even if they'd wanted to.

"I'll help," said Gary. "Let's write out a short reply in English and then you can translate it. Just a few words at a time, okay?"

"Sure." I sighed, fingering my empty coffee cup. My stomach growled.

Patrick scooted his chair away from the table and stood up. "Do you guys really need me to help with this?"

"What? You're leaving us?" Gary narrowed his eyes.

I poked Gary in the ribs before he could say something rude to Patrick. After all, he was our boss and I hoped that would still be the case on Monday, because, you know, I need to buy groceries and stuff.

"Don't worry, I'm going to make a food run," said Patrick. "I'm coming back. I don't know that I can add anything of use to your translation, so I might as well do something useful."

"Thanks," I said, genuinely appreciating the gesture. Patrick suggested a few restaurants and we decided on sandwiches to keep it simple. He refused to take our money, insisting on paying for dinner.

"Well, I'm glad he's gone," said Gary.

"You don't like Patrick much, do you?"

"He makes me sweat. I mean, I never know what he's thinking. At least the two of us get some work done."

We turned back to our task. The first short message I translated was basically acknowledging that we had understood the first one from the fireflies. I mean, from the Aelfdene. After that, we worked back and forth, first receiving a short message, translating it, and then composing a reply. We'd been at it for some time before Patrick returned with food.

I took bites of my sandwich while translating the latest message and gulped the hot coffee greedily.

"What do we have so far?" asked Patrick.

Gary snickered. "You won't believe it."

Patrick raised an eyebrow. "Yesterday I wouldn't have believed that fireflies could send messages."

"Well, the Aelfdene used to be a fey people—fairies," I explained. "They were cursed by Lucifer after they'd failed to deliver on a bargain and he stripped their magic away. He allowed them to keep their lights but turned them into insects."

"Lucifer? *The* Lucifer? Are we in danger?" Sweat sheened on Patrick's brow, despite the air conditioning.

I shook my head. "No. In fact, quite the opposite. We have something the Aelfdene want, and in return, they must offer us something of equal value."

"And that would be?" asked Patrick.

"A cure."

"They don't want to be insects," said Gary.

"Okay," said Patrick. He pushed his empty food wrappers into a paper bag, stalling for time while he thought about what to say next. I waited patiently; Gary tapped his fingers on the table.

"They believe we have a cure," I said. "And they want us to administer it to them."

"We do? And how do we know this?"

"Well..." I glanced at Gary and read back through the messages. I knew Patrick wasn't going to like what I had to say. "We've been using a catalyst to stimulate luciferin production and that is apparently weakening the magic bonds that are holding the Aelfdene in their insect forms."

"We spray them with more of the catalyst," said Gary. "Give them baths in it."

"That catalyst is an expensive item," protested Patrick. "I've told you repeatedly to stop wasting it, and I'm not authorizing you to waste more of it now."

I cringed. Patrick *had* told us to stop using it, but it had worked for our experiments—and wasn't he always the one griping about getting results?

"It's not a waste," said Gary. "It will free the fairies."

"Do you have any idea of how stupid that sounds?" said Patrick, entering full-blown boss mode.

Gary and I both just looked at him.

Patrick rubbed his neck. "Okay, it's not stupid. Not seeing this." He waved his hand at the messages and toward the lab. "How much of the catalyst do you need? I have to keep this lab on budget, you know."

"We don't exactly know," I said. "We can administer a spray to some of the fire—Aelfdene—and see how much it takes. We don't have to, er, change them all back at once."

"Very well," said Patrick. "Tell them we don't have a lot of the spray. Make sure they understand we aren't trying to trick them. I don't want Lucifer on my ass."

I raised my eyebrow. For someone who thought this whole thing sounded stupid a moment ago, Patrick was acting quite superstitious. I neglected to tell him that Lucifer was long, long ago out of the picture as far as the Aelfdene were concerned. Let him worry a bit; it would keep him off *our* asses.

I composed another message and Gary sent it to the fireflies. In short order we'd arranged to treat a control group with the catalyst. The victims—ha, ha! made you wince!—the test subjects separated themselves from the rest of the fireflies and moved to the edge of the lab table. I allowed Gary to take the spray bottle from me, thinking that this gesture might make up for his defiant act of unplugging the webcam earlier this afternoon. I was a bit surprised, though, at how eagerly Gary accepted the bottle and turned it toward the fireflies. Without further ado, he sprayed them gently with the catalyst.

Nothing happened.

"What's wrong? Why isn't anything happening?" said Patrick.

"Give it some time," I said, wishing that my boss would leave again.

"Maybe they need more." Gary spritzed the fireflies again, this time allowing the catalyst to soak them. Beads of the liquid rolled off their brown backs and puddled on the countertop.

"Don't drown them, Gary!"

"Don't waste the catalyst!" scolded Patrick.

"They're fine," said Gary, ignoring Patrick's outburst. "Look. Look!"

One of the fireflies seemed to be melting. I gasped and was unable to tear my gaze away from it. The brown wing coverings lost their shine and became fuzzy, and the center pair of legs dissolved. The insect fell and rolled over, only to sit up. What appeared to be a small *person* sat on the counter where the firefly had been. He? She? I couldn't tell, it was so small, but the fairy was wearing a brown cloth cape, yellow breeches, and a red hood, echoing the colors of the firefly.

"Hello." I leaned toward the little person and spoke quietly, afraid my voice would be too loud.

"Good day," said the fairy, climbing to its feet, which were clad with soft brown boots.

I continued to peer at the fairy, trying not to squeal with delight. Beside me I could hear Gary's sharp intake of breath. And then a loud thump caught my attention. I spun, instantly on the defensive.

Patrick was laying on the floor. He'd passed out. I decided that leaving him there was the best option. I winked at Gary, and neither of us moved to revive our boss.

"Pray tell, what has befallen him?" asked the fairy. Its voice sounded concerned and I felt a little bit of chagrin.

"He's okay. I mean, he ... well, he fainted." I had no idea if the fairy understood, but it didn't ask any more questions about Patrick.

"What is your name?" I asked. "Are you Aelfdene?"

"*We* are Aelfdene. It is the name of our people. You may call me Belenos."

We exchanged names and a few more pleasantries, and then Belenos turned to more serious issues. He told the story of the curse in more detail while Gary and I pulled up chairs to listen. For a small person, Belenos had a strong voice.

I was struck by a sudden thought once I realized that Gary wasn't having any trouble understanding Belenos. "Why are you speaking Modern English now? Your earlier messages were in Middle English."

"An odd question." Belenos cocked his head and smiled broadly. "That is more of our magic. Often the written word does not catch up to our spoken language. Is it the same with you?"

I nodded. I wasn't sure what he was referring to, just maybe how language changes faster than dictionaries and writing can keep up.

"Well," said Belenos. "I thank you for freeing me from Lucifer's curse and ask that you lift the curse for the rest of my people. I will offer you something of great value in exchange for this boon."

"Gold?" asked Gary.

Belenos turned to him. "If that is your wish."

"No, wait!" I cried. There had to be something more valuable to us than that. And I knew the old stories about fairies—Belenos would give us just enough gold to fulfill his promise without providing us with anything of real value. I didn't relish the thought of arguing with Gary and Patrick over who got to keep the teensy speck of gold.

Behind me, I heard Patrick stir. I turned to watch him for a moment. Maybe I should have revived him earlier, but he didn't appear unharmed.

"What's going on?" Patrick rubbed the back of his head

and came over to the counter. I briefly explained that we were bargaining with Belenos over our reward for lifting the curse on the Aelfdene.

"Gold," said Patrick, without a pause.

"NO!" I slid to my feet. "Patrick, Gary, please let me handle this. I think I know of something that will be much more valuable to us."

The men stared at me. Patrick wasn't used to me arguing with him. "You are the Queen here?" asked Belenos. "You seem to be the one to give orders."

I bit back a laugh. "I'm in charge of the lab, yes." I shot a warning glance at Patrick. He was technically in charge of *us*, not the lab. That was my job. I motioned for the guys to step back and give me some room. It would probably be best if just one of us dealt with the Aelfdene.

"Very well, ask for what you will." Belenos drew himself up to his full height. "But I will not deliver on my promise until after all of my people have been freed."

"You have my word," I said, praying that he wasn't about to deceive me. I bent and spoke in a low voice so the others wouldn't hear what I asked for.

Belenos looked confused. "That is your wish? It is such a small thing."

"It's of value to us," I answered. I saw Gary and Patrick watching me, but I clamped my mouth shut. Let them wonder what I'd asked for.

We spent the rest of the evening spraying fireflies with the catalyst. By the end of the night we had a lab full of fairies. Some danced with glee, others sang, and many just flew around the room for joy. Eventually Belenos gathered his people together to bid us farewell.

"But what about ...?" I started.

Belenos smiled. "You have my word that I will deliver on my promise. Two days' hence, you will have what you value most." He sketched a formal bow, and then all of the Aelfdene took to the air and flew out of the lab.

"What did you ask him for?" said Patrick.

"I don't want to tell you yet," I said. "But it will be worth more than fairy gold. Just wait." I put on a brave front, but I couldn't be sure that Belenos would keep his part of the bargain. I didn't want the guys to know how I felt, so I pleaded having a headache and left them standing in the kitchenette.

It was late, and the stars were out when I reached the parking lot. The building's back door was still off its hinges, but I'd let Patrick deal with the building supervisor. That's what bosses are for. I got in my car and went home.

* * *

All day Sunday I worried about the lab, but I refused to answer the phone when Gary and Patrick called me.

Very early Monday morning I headed in to work. The back door had been replaced, and I let myself in to the building. I got to the lab and realized I was holding my breath. I swiped my access card and pushed the door open.

I wasn't sure what I had expected, but I hadn't truly believed that Belenos would deliver on his promise. But he had!

The lab's glass wall had been replaced and behind it were the rows of terrariums. But something was different. I went closer to have a look. Each tank had a small piece of paper attached to it that indicated where the fireflies had been collected. Inside the tank, every insect was painted with a bright dot of paint. One terrarium had insects with white dots, another had pink, another had gold. I idly wondered if it were real gold, then pushed the silly thought aside.

I smiled. We were back in business.

PERIODIC MAGIC

Cathryn Leigh

Montana hung out after the game at Arizona Prep. She wasn't a big fan of football; even having watched Pele play it for the last six years didn't make her understand it anymore. Probably because he was on the field and she was opposite the bleachers, watching with no one to tell her what was going on. She never pressed Pele to explain it, either. He only played to make his father happy.

Pele's true sport was *futbul*, otherwise known as soccer. He was named for it. Had the build for it. And he loved it. But his dad thought it was okay, so Pele only got to play on World Cup years. And only because it didn't conflict with American football.

Waiting under the shade of a tree near the far side of the high school baseball diamond, Montana watched the crowd filter through. She leaned against the trunk, using it to channel her wild static energy into the ground. It had been a good game and the home team had won, but there had been a lot of close calls. And the last thing she needed was to be flagged as a dangerous Alkali.

Montana took a deep breath, pushing the memories of her mom aside. Pele's dad hadn't been in the bleachers. That meant Pele would be walking home, so Montana watched the crowd. It wasn't until the last players trickled out that she spotted him. Pele walked, laughing, with two teammates. She waited as they passed by. He barely glanced at her, but she trailed behind them anyway, maintaining a steady breath to keep her static from tagging them. It wasn't long before the group split up, most going to their cars, Pele heading to 9th Street. He paused at the corner and Montana caught up.

"You know you don't have to wait for me anymore."

Montana shrugged. "Habit."

They walked side-by-side for a block before Montana spoke up again. "Didn't see your dad tonight."

"Yeah," Pele sighed. "Work probably kept him late. Probably good though, I'm not sure he could have handled that game."

Montana snorted. "I know I had to stay grounded."

Pele laughed. It was always good to hear him laugh. "You didn't leave any scorch marks did you?"

"Hey, I only did that once," she chided him, though she ruined it by smiling. "Still," she sobered up again. "It was a win, so that's a good start to fall break, right?"

"True," Pele nodded. "Now if only the Cardinals would actually win a season game, Mom and I would be golden."

Montana nodded. She used to listen to the Phoenix baseball team's games, but then work had taken her weekends.

She still looked up the scores, and always hoped, for Pele and his mom's sake, that the Cardinals would win. They'd won almost all of their pre-season games, but were now in a losing streak from hell. Pele stopped as they reached his corner.

"The guys told me I ought to go to homecoming this year, being my senior year and all."

"Really?" A stray spark jumped from her fingertip to the ground. She clasped her hands behind her back. "Are you going stag?"

"Maybe?" He shrugged. "What about you? You going?"

Montana took a deep breath and let it out. "Maybe? Juana said the same thing, about being a high school senior and all." She snorted. "She also said I should go stag because I might meet an alumni who'd be perfect for me." She used air quotes, which left a trail of static in its wake. She hid her hands again, wishing she was nearer a tree. Trees were great at defusing her *dangerous* magic. She had no wish to go into a Powercell and never return, like her Mom.

"Tell you what," Pele's loam-brown eyes caught hers. "I'll save you a dance, in case that 'perfect' alumni doesn't show up." His air quotes were light, and way better controlled than her static.

Montana's smile grew into a devilish grin, thoughts of her mom vanishing. "If I don't get that dance at homecoming, I might have to seek you out the Prom to get one."

"Ahh," Pele threw his hands up in front of him, "don't threaten me!"

They both broke into laughter, until Pele shook his head.

"I'll see you around Tana." He waved as he started down his street.

"See ya around," she called back with a single wave.

To bad she wouldn't actually see him around. Their paths never crossed over the holidays, though she did hope to go to next Friday's game.

* * *

Trying to explain his friendship with Montana was hard. Half his team said he should just ask her out, the other half said he should just ditch her. But it was a hard habit to break, given that they'd been friends since second grade. Pele shook the thoughts from his head as he opened the door to their apartment. Pele set his bag down by the door and called out to his mom.

"We won."

"Dinner is in fifteen minutes," she responded.

"Setting the table, then."

Pele put his words to action so that dinner was ready the moment his dad walked in the door. And he did with a smile on his face.

"Heard about your win," his dad slapped Pele on the back as he hung his suit jacket in their tiny coat closet. "It's all about teamwork, maybe you guys can pull it together for the season."

"We will," Pele replied, despite knowing that this win was a fluke.

They sat down as his mom placed a cold beer in front of his dad. The man took an immediate sip and sighed. His mom served them both before herself. Pele waited for her to sit down. His dad did not. Between bites, his dad shot questions about the game to Pele. Pele answered as best he could, doing his best to glide over the penalties and setbacks that had occurred.

Grunting, his dad made a few passing remarks about the plays they chose, and then complained his steak wasn't cooked right. Pele's mom only reply was a "Yes, dear," as she kept her eyes on the table and her head bowed. She ate slowly and Pele remained seated when his dad rose. He would wait until she was done; his dad, however, grabbed another cold beer from the fridge before heading to the living room.

From his chair, Pele watched his dad flop into the recliner. The one piece of furniture that remained pristine, due to his mom's efforts of daily cleaning and restoring. The rest of the house suffered for it. The shabby couch covered with thrift store sheets, rotated and turned until there were no unburnt spots and then replaced with another set. His dad once complained that he couldn't bring his friends over anymore as they were starting to talk about what a wreck it was.

His mom had done nothing about that comment. His dad went out more often. Pele was glad of it.

Standing as his mother placed her knife and fork down, Pele began to clear the table. He scraped the dishes, rinsed them, and stacked them neatly. He put away the leftovers and prepped the sink for washing dishes as his mom finished her quarter-glass of wine.

"Boy," his dad called from his chair, back to them, "stop doing your mom's work. Come in here and get your fantasy football team stats."

"In a moment, Dad."

Pele learned long ago the proper responses to his father. Yelling back did no good, despite the fact that somedays he wished he could have a Montana-sized moment of losing control. He'd tried that once. Once. Pele pushed the memory down, trying to focus on the positive. His mom stood and kissed him on the cheek. Pele smiled at her, leaning down slightly to kiss her forehead.

"Well boy?" His dad called, "how's your fantasy football team doing?"

Pele entered the living room and picked up his bag. He pulled out his phone as he sunk into the couch. He ought to find a board somewhere so the couch didn't sink when you sat on it. He wrinkled his nose at his stats.

"Ha!" His dad grinned, a wild light in his eye. "I got you this time."

"Yeah, Dad," Pele intoned as he set his phone down, "you really did." *Because I picked my team to be weaker than yours.*

Leaning over, Pele pulled his biology homework for the holidays. His father grunted.

"Don't see why you got to study that. Medical stuff ought to be left to the Non-Metals."

"It was required, Dad." Pele used the rhetoric he always used, even when it was an elective he'd chosen. Just because his magic was classified as Halogen and thus more *fitted* to a trades skill like wielding didn't mean he couldn't become a doctor if he wanted to. Just like Tana didn't have to be a Powercell just because she was alkali.

His dad set his beer down on the table by his chair. Before he could yell to the kitchen, Pele's mom was replacing it with a new one. His dad smirked and took a swig. He grimaced.

"Too cold."

"Yes dear," Pele's mom replied, though she did nothing.

Pele replaced biology with math to stall the storm. Being an accountant, math was his dad's favorite subject, even if he hadn't figured out common core. So Pele did it the way his dad showed him. Later, when his dad was at work, Pele'd redo it the way the teacher had taught it.

* * *

Just because she had no school didn't mean that Montana could avoid her control sessions at Banner University Medical Center. The first real day of break found Montana reclined on a rubber couch in a concrete room, glaring at the thick glass separating her from Doctor Wolfy. Her body crackled and zapped as she took deep breaths, taming her roiling emotions.

Control.

That was her desire.

Control.

Stop her electric fire.

Control.

A chuckle escaped her as the crackles dissipated.

"And vat trick did you use?" Dr. Wolfy's voice sounded like her static.

"A song, rhyme, thing." Montana grinned. She snapped her fingers in a rhythm as she tapped her toes.

"Control," she snapped with a spark, "that's my desire. Control," another sparking snap. "Stops my electric fire. Control." She snapped but kept it from sparking.

"Zat is good." Dr. Wolfy's smile lit his face. "Vee just need some beat boxing and vee vill have a number-vone hit."

Montana laughed, sending skittering sparks against her chest where she slapped it with her hands. She breathed deep again. Control was hard. Maybe if she was a Vulkan alkali mage. But she was only human. A human with strong emotions and the ability to swing from one extreme to another. At least Dr. Wolfy had figured out the emotional connection early on. Now they had to figure out how to disconnect them from her volatile power.

And if he could do that with her, other alkalis wouldn't suffer her mom's fate—sent to the electric plant to become a Powercell for the city. Maybe they'd find a way to make it something you could survive, something an alkali could volunteer to do.

"I think vee are done today." The Doctor's voice crackeld into her thoughts. "You may remove zee sensors."

Montana complied, gently stripping off the rubber bands that encircled her wrists, ankles, and head. Then she undid the odd belt from her torso. If it were stiffer she'd have called it a corset, but the rubber stretched and was way more comfortable than one might expect a sensor-containing device to be. She set them all on the couch, knowing Dr. Wolfy would be in to download the data and clean them once she left.

He smiled as she approached the door that led from the static room to his office. It had been especially designed to contain the electrical magic of alkali mages.

"Zat vas a good session." He gave her a hug, her residual charge making him look like Doc from *Back to the Future*. "You have improved greatly."

"Well, I hope so." Montana returned the hug. "It's been twelve years." She smiled to take the sass out of her words.

"I vill miss you ven you graduate. You are my prize research project."

Montana chuckled. "Just remember," she grabbed her backpack. "I want a signed copy of the article, and when you win the Nobel Peace Prize I better be invited." She shouldered her pack and opened the outer office door. "Catch you next week."

"And remember," he waved her out.

"Stay calm." They spoke in unison as she closed the door.

A student ran into her as she rounded a corner, his papers scattering. Drained from the session with Dr. Wolfy, she stumbled. "Native American symbology as it..." was all she could read before the student whisked it away. She watched as he entered Dr. Wolfy's office and shook her head. She knew she wasn't his only research project, yet she always felt special in his office. Sessions with him had become a sanctuary. A calm in the craziness of her life. If only she had enough control to watch Pele's away games. Not that he seemed to want her at the home games anymore.

Sighing with the bus as its hydraulics lowered the right side, Montana texted her guardian that she was on her way home. Not that the woman cared, just so long as the government gave her money for housing Montana and that Montana didn't electri-fry anything.

* * *

Football practice continued through the fall break. There was a home game scheduled for Friday. There was something eerie about being in the school with no one else. And yet Pele would often hang back in the locker room, just to be the last one out. Just to be alone, to feel free for just a moment until the loneliness was about to swallow him whole.

Then he'd be outside with the rest of the crew, joking and laughing until one by one they drove home. And Pele would walk home, always declining the rides offered by his teammates and his coach.

"It's not that far," he'd always say, "helps me stay fit for soccer."

But it wasn't the walk that kept him fit. It was the list of things to do that his dad gave him the first day of break.

"Don't dally, I expect it all done."

It wasn't just his dad's list. Years ago his dad had pimped Pele's fix-it services to the neighbors, raking in all the dough that Pele's hard work earned. Pele had watched more YouTube videos on home improvement projects than homeowners twice his age. He probably completed more in a summer than a homeowner did in three years. Not hard when his dad bragged about his son's skills to coworkers, while berating Pele for shoddy work. But Pele was starting to turn it around for himself.

As soon as he could, Pele got a bank account—without his dad's name on it—and had the statements sent electronically. Many of the neighborhood folks came to him directly instead of going to his dad. Pele still gave his dad a cut to keep back the storm. His customers had been willing to pay the increased prices. So Pele watched his savings grow. He was going to get out of this dry desert town one day, and he'd no plans of coming back.

"Pele Windsong," a silky voice purred. "What are you doing under my sink?"

"Fixing your plumbing," Pele grunted as he tightened the last of the O-rings.

Ducking his head as he pushed himself out from under the counter, Pele stood to face Jessica White, the hottest cheerleader of the Phoenix Prep Sun Devils.

"This is what got stuck in the garbage disposal."

Pele extended his hand, a petite diamond ring in his hand. With a touch of halogen magic he made it sparkle under the grime.

"Oohh," Jessica squealed. "Are you proposing?"

"What? No." Pele nearly closed his hand around the ring, his body heat rising. "Just returning lost property."

"Well," she picked it up with just her nails. "That's not going on my finger any time soon."

The ring jingled as it bounced on the table. She stepped closer to Pele, their bodies nearly touching. Pele could barely breathe. She leaned in, her words tickling his ear, a metallic taste filling his mouth as her finger brushed his chest.

"Anytime you want to come over and fix *my* plumbing is fine by me."

Pele swallowed, grateful his naturally copper skin hid the heat of his cheeks. Jessica turned and walked away, her shorts and top barely covering enough skin to be lawful. She'd reached the kitchen door when he blurted out, "Do you want to go to Homecoming with me?"

Jessica turned with a brilliant smile. "Why Pele, I thought you'd never ask."

"That was a yes, right?" he called as the front door opened.

Her musical laughter floated back. Pele signed as he turned back to the sink. He cleaned up and packed his tools, giving Mr. White a rundown of what happened regarding the garbage disposal. The man furrowed his brows then shook his head and paid Pele for his work. Walking home, Pele wondered if Jessica was setting him up for something. Then again he *was* on the football team, just like all her past boyfriends. So Pele figured he'd find out next game.

* * *

It felt like Montana had just closed her eyes when her phone rang. Working nights restocking shelves at Costco made her thankful for school vacation. She peered at her phone. It was still ringing. With a groan she picked it up.

"Montana, where are you?" Juana's voice accosted her over the line. "You promised to go dress shopping with me."

"Juana," Montana closed her eyes, "I'm exhausted, if you don't want me to blow out any lights give me until noon."

"Fine." Juana made a disgusted noise. "But you better be there!"

"Text the location, I'll take a bus." Montana hung up before Juana could go on to another topic. She turned "do not disturb" on and let her phone plop back on her desk. Rolling over, she let out a deep breath, and some static, and fell asleep.

Three hours later Montana was up. Her guardian was not. Montana was never sure if the woman worked, or if she just lived off the money the state gave her for housing Montana. Housing was about all she got. If it wasn't for Abuelita Rosita, the apartment grandmother, Montana would have starved. She didn't really care that working nights meant she got tomalitos for breakfast. They were delicious any time of day.

"And where are you off to today?" Rosalita served Montana another tomalito from her never-ending supply. Seriously, Montana was sure that's all the ancient woman ever did.

"Dress shopping for Homecoming."

"Oh, are you going with that friend of yours?"

"Pele?" Montana snorted as Rosalita nodded. "Naw, don't think he likes me that way. I just figured I should go."

"Well I'm sure he'll see what a sweetheart you are before the Prom." Abuelita Rosalita patted Montana's cheek.

Montana stood and kissed the woman's wrinkled

forehead. She grabbed some cash from her stash that Abuelita kept for her and headed out. Montana had tried keeping money in her room, but she'd soon discovered that her guardian pilfered it. With wall-to-wall carpeting, Montana couldn't do a classic floorboard hiding spot either. Seriously, who carpets closets?

Practicing her mantra, Montana waited for the bus.

Control. That's my desire. Control. To stop my electric fire. Control.

Juana could kiss dress shopping goodbye if Montana couldn't control her static. For some reason stores didn't appreciate it when their clothing clung to their customers in unflattering ways. At least Juana was a good sport about getting kicked out. She always managed to spot the funniest of the clings that she'd describe in such great detail that Montana always had to laugh. Together they wondered how alkalis born before the internet managed to survive. Montana had to get all her school uniforms online—even Goodwill didn't like to have her in their stores.

She arrived at Macy's, one she hadn't been kicked out of yet, to find Juana waiting for her with fifteen bags in hand.

"What in the world did you do, buy all of the dresses?" Montana laughed.

Juana didn't smile. "And some in two sizes." She shoved some bags at Montana. "Come on, we're going to my house to try them on, I can return them all after Homecoming."

"Um, okay." Montana took the bags and trailed after Juana.

Her trunk was already full of bags so they had to stick them in the back seat of her clunker. Montana paused, hand on the open passenger side door.

"Are you sure you want to drive me? I can short circuit even the newest of cars."

"Oh, get in and stop fussing." Juana slid into the driver's seat. "My brother wants to see if his retro static control works."

"He's still working on that project?"

"Of course he is." Juana started the ignition as Montana whispered her mantra.

"He knows there's a tiny market for it, right?" Montana broke her mantra as they merged onto the highway.

Juana just waved her hand at Montana as if that didn't matter. Buses, they had been built to better withstand the potential accidental (or conscious) discharge of magic. Which is why Montana would be more comfortable on one of them than in this ancient beast of a car. It was probably from the early 2000s or something. Montana sat on her hands, continually chanting her mantra as Juana babbled on about this project and that. All things her genius mechanical brother was working on at MIT. Montana wondered what it was like so far away on the East Coast. She'd seen the pictures of Boston that Juana's brother posted online.

"Wait, what was that?" Montana asked as Juana dropped a bomb in her blathering.

They pulled onto Juana's street.

"Raul said he saw Pele and Jessica 'hanging out' after practice."

The air quotes didn't miss Montana. "Making out, you mean."

She clasped her hands, squeezing them together, as the car spluttered.

Control. That's my desire. Control. To stop my electric fire. Control.

"We-e-ell," Juana drew out the syllables as they coasted into the driveway and she put the car in park. She gripped the steering wheel. "Raul just said she was wrapped around his arm."

"Whatever." Montana slowly unclenched her hands, releasing each finger one by one, watching them intently.

Juana popped the trunk as her little sister Maria bounded to the car. "You buy the whole store?" The little girl's eyes were wide.

"I asked the same question," Montana grumbled.

Juana shook her head at both of them. "No. We are going to make Montana look so beautiful that Pele won't be able to think of anyone else."

Montana opened her mouth to protest, but Juana's "I mean business" stare shut her up. Instead, she grabbed as many bags as she could and trailed after Juana and her sister. She wasn't sure she'd ever be able to compete with the *beauty* that was Jessica White.

* * *

Pele's horrible practice was only tempered by the fact that Jessica was standing right next to him. So close that somehow he found his arm had managed to end up around her waist. He'd expected her to want to discuss when he'd pick her up for Homecoming. He was actually surprised she hadn't already had a date. And now, here she was acting very much like a girlfriend.

Inside his stomach was churning like it did when he walked home in the rain after a lost game. Outside he smiled, laughed, and joked. Tried to act like he was a part of the "taken" crew. Girls hanging on their boys, talking dresses, while the boys discussed football. But Pele could feel time ticking. Could sense that he needed to leave, but he didn't know how to extricate himself.

The bag at his feet vibrated with the muffled ring tone that meant time was up. Trying to untangle himself from Jessica he rummaged for his phone. She pouted at him.

"Sorry, it's my dad."

"Forget your dad," she purred, clinging tighter.

"I wish I could," he sighed, glancing to her crystal blue eyes. "But he's pretty strict."

"Iron-tight fist, that man," one of his team mates commented.

"Yeah, so bad, you're actually his first girlfriend," another chuckled.

Pele froze, certain Jessica would ditch him then and there. She just wrapped her arms around his neck and smiled. He felt his stomach plummet.

"So I'm your first?" she whispered, licking her lips. "Don't worry," she whispered into his ear, "I'll show you all the moves you need to know."

She stepped back, her hands traveling down his chest. They lingered to where his charm hung. He felt tired. A metallic taste parched his mouth. Then it was gone.

"See you next practice." She winked and turned from him.

Pele got to his phone at last and shouldered his bag. He texted his dad as he walked home.

/On my way home. Practice ran late. Phone was buried./

He prayed there was no storm brewing at home. This was why he'd never had a girlfriend before. Why his friendship with Montana was based on a mutual walk to and from school.

"Practice didn't run long, boy." His dad's greeting was not friendly as Pele opened the door.

"Yeah, it did, Dad," *by a few minutes at least.* Pele tried to get past, but his father blocked the way.

"You was done when I drove by. Where were you?"

Pele cringed. "Hanging out with the team. And the cheerleaders." He added as an afterthought.

Pele's dad stepped from the doorway, giving Pele access to the house. Pele's mom knelt on the living room carpet, a pile of brown broken glass beside her.

"And why'd you do that when you haven't before, eh boy?"

Pele moved past his dad, collecting his thoughts as his father closed the door. It was a deliberate closing, so Pele thought about his words really carefully.

"Answer me, boy."

Pele still remained silent, knowing he was only delaying the inevitable, making it worse. But he was tired of being followed, watched like a hawk, and for what?

"Pele?" His mother's voice pleaded from the living room.

Heaving a deep breath, Pele turned to face his steaming father.

"Well, boy?"

"I've got a girlfriend."

His dad stepped back as if Pele was some sort of alien. "A cheerleader?"

"The head cheerleader." Pele stood taller. So what if he wasn't the quarterback, so what if he was the last person on the team she hadn't dated. So what if she was setting him up to fall.

His dad blinked, then a smile crept onto his face. Pele stepped back as his dad stepped over. His dad was *smiling*?

"Lead cheerleader, huh?" Pele nodded. "That's my boy!" He slapped Pele on the back. "Woman! Get us some beers, my boy's becoming a man."

"Yes, dear."

Pele carefully stepped around the spot his mom had been cleaning. He sank into the couch, taking the bottle from her, mouthing a silent thank you when he smelled the root beer. He clinked glasses with his dad, knowing that a few beers in the man could be cursing him just as easily as he was praising him.

"You got to bring that girl over for dinner," his dad nodded. "Woman, you can make the house look good for that, can't you?"

"Yes, dear."

Pele desperately wanted to set his beer down and help her clean, but years of hard discipline had trained him to never do that in the presence of his father. So for now he enjoyed the calm.

* * *

The best part about a vacation game day was that Montana got to sleep in, see Dr. Wolfy, and watch Pele play. She'd prefer soccer, but that season was still two months away. She wondered if Jessica had ever watched a soccer game, or was she a football-only girl? Not that it mattered. Damn Juana for putting it into Montana's head that she was in some sort of competition with the prettiest, most popular, and sluttiest, girl of the school. Besides, Juana had only repeated what Raul had said, and Raul wasn't always reliable. Going to the game meant Montana could verify the rumor for herself.

The idea of Pele dating Jessica was absurd. She was their nemesis in grade school. Okay, maybe she was only

Montana's nemesis, but had he forgotten how she'd stolen the pendant his grandfather had given him? That's the whole reason they became friends. Montana had gotten it back for him. Still, the memory of Jessica's Franken-bride hair after that encounter never failed to make Montana smile. Little second-grade Jessica had claimed trauma, that it'd taken her weeks to recover her hair and months to recover her sanity.

Control. That's my desire. Control. To stop my electric fire. Control.

Jessica knew nothing about trauma or sanity.

Control. That's my desire. Control. To stop my electric fire. Control.

Montana practiced releasing tension as she walked up to Dr. Wolfy's office. She rolled her shoulders, knocked on the doorframe, and entered. He glanced up from his studies and waved her over excitedly.

"I zink I've got it!" This time he caught her eyes, his whole face smiling.

"Got what?" Montana furrowed her brows, trying to figure out what he was reading. She set her bag down.

"Did you know," the doctor's nose was once more burred in the book. "Zee Native Americans found a vay to temper alkali magic? All other forms, too."

"No." Montana shook her head, placing her hands on his desk. She'd seen the book before, Native American symbology, the one the student dropped in the hall.

"Amulets." He rotated the book so that she could clearly see picture. "Zey used zee arcane symbols, often seen in medieval literature. But somehow zey knew how to turn zee amulet into some sort of channeling and dampening device."

The picture showed three wooden disks, each carved

with a different arcane symbol. An equilateral triangle, point upwards, dissected by a vertical line was captioned.

"The pendant acted like a grounding device for its alkali owner," she read aloud. She looked at Dr. Wolfy. "How do I get one?"

"Ah, vell," the brilliance faded from his face, "Zat is my current quandary."

Montana flopped into the chair in front of his desk. "Well at least I have my mantra from last week. It's helped, some."

"It has?"

She nodded.

"Good, good."

"Anything I can do to help figure out how to get me an amulet, though?"

Dr. Wolfy let out a long sigh. "Zat really is zee question. Zee few sources I have found covering zese charms indicate zey were made by shaman, and zat zey are specific to an individual."

Montana stared at the other pendants on the page. One was just an equilateral triangle pointing up, the symbol for metalloids. The third, aside from her own symbol, was the circle of a noble gas. That struck Montana as funny since noble gases had no magic. In fact they were immune to it, which is why Juana had no issue hanging out with Montana. Montana could go haywire, and Juana would be fine.

"I have my grad students, "Dr. Wolfy broke her thoughts, "looking to find a shaman, or any Native American, voo knows more."

Montana nodded, glancing once more at the photo of the pendants dug up from some gravesite in New Mexico. There was something familiar about them, but she couldn't' quite place it. It bugged her all through the session, which strangely helped her control. It even bugged her into the game until the announcer called Pele's number.

She nearly shocked herself for not thinking of it sooner. But then she'd only truly seen Pele's pendant once, and that was when she'd gotten it back from Jessica and handed it to him. If only she'd known then what she knew now. She'd still have given the pendant back. But if it was individualized, and if it was tuned to Pele, what would happen if he gave it to Jessica?

Montana gripped the tree behind her, praying that Raul's rumor was not true, not true at all.

* * *

Jessica pulled Pele from the group and around a corner of the building. She pulled him in close, covering his lips with her own. Pele couldn't enjoy it. Not when the game had gone so far south. He tried. He tried to get into the caresses and kisses, tried to return the favor, but the metallic taste in his mouth made him pull back. Jessica had pulled his pendant from under his shirt and stroked it.

"Don't you think I'd look pretty with that on?"

Pele looked at the dingy wooden disk. "No, you're way prettier than it."

She laughed. It sounded like bells. "Then why do *you* wear it?"

"My granddad gave it to me." Pele pulled it from her grasp and tucked it back into his shirt.

"Mmm." She was kissing him again, fingers curling around his body parts.

"Jessica," he lifted her head from his chest. "I have to go."

"Ugh," She took his head in her hands, giving him one last long kiss. "You *will* stay after Homecoming. Promise?"

"Promise," he heaved.

She walked away laughing. He walked away trying to figure out what to tell his dad that would allow him to keep that promise. Maybe "Dad I'm trying to get laid?" Hah.

"So," Montana's voice hit him as he turned up 9th Street. "You really are dating Jessica White."

Pele kept walking. "Jealous?" The word was out before he thought.

"What?" She'd caught up to him. "No," she snorted. "More like disappointed."

"That I didn't ask you?" Again words without thought. Was he hoping that Montana was jealous?

Montana slapped her hands to her face, with a muttered argh. "That you asked Jessica. Jessica *White*."

"Oh right." It hit him like a ton of bricks. "You two don't get along."

"More like she's my mortal enemy," Montana corrected.

His arm hairs stood on end as Montana clasped one sparking hand with the other. He kept walking fast, wanting this conversation to be over. She caught up.

"But really, Pele, you're too good for her."

Pele stopped and turned to face his friend. Once upon a time she'd been his only friend. He blinked. "How?" He frowned at her. "Her dad hires me to fix things in his house. She's already got more money than I'll ever make in my lifetime. Not to mention she's, well, smoking hot."

"And you're not?" Montana rolled her eyes. "But taking looks out of the equation. She's selfish, manipulative, and most likely using you to drive her dad loco."

"What if she actually likes me, Tana?" Pele countered, "Have you factored that in?"

"Even if she does," Montana admitted, "she's still using you. She doesn't know how not to."

Montana pivoted and walked back down the block. Pele furrowed his brows, watching her for a moment. He wasn't an insecure little kid any more. Pele jogged homeward. He didn't need Montana's protection anymore. He glanced back as he turned onto his street, expecting to see Montana rushing back his way to catch her bus. But she wasn't. And he wasn't going to let her tirade against Jessica get to him.

* * *

Montana marched her way back past the school to catch the number 3 bus home. It seemed she'd been taking this bus home more often as of late. As soon as she was plopped into a seat she texted Juana.

/Raul was right/

/Wha?/

/Pele and Jessica.*eyeroll emoji*/

/Jealous? *laughing emoji*/

/No *mad devil emoji*/

/U sure?/

/He's better than that *exclamation point emoji*/

/She _is_ hot *flame emoji*/

Montana rolled her eyes and stared at the buildings of businesses and apartments, the Phoenix skyline never higher than three stories. Beyond them were single-story homes in small patches of brown yards, with the occasional flash of greenery. Someday Montana would find a way out of this dry hellhole. Someday.

Montana slapped her forehead. She'd completely forgotten to ask Pele about his pendant. If Dr. Wolfy was right, that would be her ticket to freedom. Sure, she'd graduate his program when she graduated high school. There wasn't a college around that accepted alkalis. At least nothing anywhere near her price range. And even if there was, she'd still be watched. She'd still be stuck on night shift, restocking shelves. Always alone in the aisle, warning signs hung at either ends.

Heaven help her if she fell out of line, just one tiny bit. Alkali weren't even given benefit of the doubt in a trial. If you electrocuted someone you became a Powercell. Montana wrapped her arms around herself and shivered. She would not be like her mom. She couldn't. Not that she'd be leaving a kid behind, parentless. Still...

Shaking the morbidity away, Montana pulled out her phone as she got off at her stop. She stayed there for a moment, pulling up her text history with Pele. She blinked away her gathering tears. Their last text had been almost two years ago, end of tenth grade. Promises they'd never made because they knew they couldn't keep them.

/Sorry *single tear sad emoji*/

Montana checked each day of break, but Pele didn't reply. At least today, a Thursday of all days, they went back to school. Just in time to have two days of nothing but Homecoming preparations. Montana normally just skipped these days, but she wanted to make sure Pele knew that, no mater what, Montana was still his friend. But he barely glanced her way that day.

Friday morning, she hazarded another text.

/Pele? *O.o emoji*/

Not a peep from him. She should probably just give up. Maybe try again, after football was over. Maybe he'd have come to his senses by then.

"You know," a silky serpent voice whispered in her ear. "I

don't like you texting my boyfriend."

Montana glanced to Jessica. "I don't like you dating my friend."

Jessica snorted, leaning against the lockers. Five other girls surrounded them. "Give it up *Tana*."

The hair raised on the back of Montana's neck at Jessica's use of Pele's nickname for her. Jessica continued before she could respond to that.

"If he hasn't asked you out yet, he *never* will. So you can drop that whole *friend* pretense."

Montana slammed her locker, bolts of lightning skittering across it. "I *am* his friend and while I don't like the thought of you two dating, if that's what he wants, then fine. But," Montana stepped forward, leaning in until her nose was millimeters from Jessica's, "I will remain his friend, whether you like it or not."

A single spark jumped between their noses. Jessica stumbled back, hand over her nose. "Ow, you hurt me." She turned on the fake tears. "I can't believe you did that, you all saw her attack me didn't you?" Her cronies nodded. "Pele!"

Montana caught sight of him, just turning the corner. She closed her eyes and took a deep breath. *Control. That's my desire. Control. To stop my electric fire. Control.* The moment she opened them, Montana regretted it. Jessica was clinging to Pele, her nose still covered, sobbing to the principal. Jessica's talent of making mountains out of molehills irked Montana to no end.

Control. That's my desire. Control. To stop my electric fire. Control.

"It doesn't look that bad." The principal's words filtered through. "However, Montana."

She focused on the principal's face.

"You will be banned from all Homecoming activities, including tonight's game."

Montana's eyes flicked to Jessica's smirk, her hand pressed against Pele's chest. Fingers clutching the pendant under his clothing. Montana tensed her whole body, keeping her emotions in as much as she could.

"Fine," she told the principal. She made eye contact with Pele. "I always preferred soccer."

Storming from the school, Montana continued her chant. *Control. That's my desire. Control. To stop my electric fire. Control.* Her body stayed wound as tightly as a spring no matter how many time she said it. But she kept it wound, fists balled, lips sealed, until she'd had on all the sensors and she was in the static chamber. And then she screamed.

* * *

Pele watched Montana storm off. "Why?" He looked at Jessica, who clung to him like he was some sort of life raft.

"Didn't you see her hurt me?" Jessica cajoled. "Look at my nose!"

Pele looked at it. Looked at her. Fought the copper taste in his mouth. Was she really crying? He kissed Jessica's nose.

"All better?"

She laughed. "Oh, Pele, I need better kisses than that."

Inwardly he groaned. "Not here, not now, and..." he stared into her eyes. "I want you to be nicer to Tana. She *is* my friend."

Jessica pouted. "Fine." She gave him a quick kiss to the lips. "Good luck at tonight's game."

Pele ran his hands through his hair as she walked off with her gaggle of girls. They needed more than luck tonight. The team needed to pull it together. Not even the coach's promise of a pizza party was enough motivation for this group. It'd worked great in junior varsity, but the varsity boys, the seniors, all they wanted was booze and cheerleaders. And neither they, nor the girls, seemed to mind being passed about so long as someone's fake ID worked to procure the alcohol.

If only it were soccer season. Pele longed for his soccer team. Maybe they weren't champions, but they were a team. And they played like one, too. Sitting on the bleachers, he watched the junior varsity football players practice. Even though it was three hours between the end of school and the game, he preferred not to go home. So his mom just packed extra in his lunch.

The older players began to filter in as the younger one drifted off the field, cheerleaders hanging off their arms. Jessica wasn't with them. Nor had she materialized to cling to him. A part of him was glad. She clung to him, grabbed him, kissed him in public as if she needed to make sure everyone knew he was hers. Like the way his dad always had his mom right next to him, touching him, when they went out in public.

Pulling out his phone to check the time, Pele decided to text Montana. Jessica would never apologize, but he could. He scrolled through his text history. He knew he'd texted her before. He tried to type in her name but neither Montana or Tana pulled up anything. He searched his contacts. Nothing.

Coach yelled for them to come in, and Pele saw the first of the opposing team's buses pull in. He shoved his phone in his bag and jogged to the locker room. They could win this if they tried!

Or...

Or they could lose by a landslide, making this the worst Homecoming game in their school's history. Pele took way longer in the shower than he meant to. He didn't want to go home. His dad would be livid. He should tell Jessica to forget about Homecoming. His sneakered feet made little noise in the linoleum halls. Voices in the emptiness made Pele stop. He held his breath, cautiously creeping closer. There were grunts and moans. They paused for breathless words.

"Ain't your boyfriend still in the locker room?"

"That dork?" a laugh, Jessica's laugh. "He's either gay or strict Catholic. I can barely get him to put his hands on me."

Pele peeked around the corner only to reel back. He leaned on the lockers, trying to steady himself.

"And I can barely keep my hands off you."

The male voice was followed by grunts and moans. Pele gagged, quickly turning and storming down the hall. He burst open the doors with a flash bang of bright light. The few people outside jumped, took one look at him, and stepped back.

"PELE!"

Jessica's heels echoed in the corridors. Pele kept walking, letting the doors slam shut in her face.

"Pele!"

He stared straight ahead, ignoring the pleading voice behind him. If only he had a car and could drive away. He'd drive far away from here, never look back. Fuck school.

"Pele?"

Jessica was right behind him, so he stopped. Pivoting, he stared at her, hard, cold. She stepped back.

"What?" he growled.

"It's not what you think."

Were those even real tears in her eyes?

"Not what I think?" He stared hard at her. "Do you even care what I think?"

"Yes," she fanned her eyes. "See, I was just talking."

"Oh right, talking. Talking with your tongue in his mouth, talking with his hands on your butt, talking like," and Pele imitated the sounds they'd been making.

Jessica at least had the decency to blush. "Pele," her voice softened to seductive. "It's you I really want, why don't you just give it to me?" She fingered his pendant as his energy drained and the copper taste invaded his mouth.

"No." He yanked the pendant from her grasp, feeling immediate relief.

"Just let me wear your pendant, and I promise I'll be good. I promise you'll be the only one."

Her hands slid around his neck, trying to undo the knot on the twine that held the wooden disk in place. He grabbed those hands and forced them to her side. He held them there and brought his face so close to hers their noses nearly touched.

"No."

Pele's dad wore his mom's pendant. Maybe that's why she never left him. Pele dropped Jessica's arms and took a long step backward.

"We're through, Jessica. Go find another dork to fuck you at Homecoming."

He turned from her and sprinted. He didn't want her to catch up, so he didn't slow down until he was two blocks from the school. He glanced back and stopped. Jessica hadn't followed. Nor, he sighed, was there any sign of Tana. Shit, he'd forgotten she'd been banned from today's game, as well as tomorrow's dance. Pulling out his phone, he also remembered Montana's number wasn't there. Continuing his walk home, Pele scrolled through his remaining contacts.

What the hell had Jessica done to his phone and when?

His dad's number wasn't there, his mom's number wasn't there. Pele fumed as he entered his house. His dad rose from his pristine chair and Pele glared at him.

"It's been a bad night, Dad," Pele spoke before his dad could. "And if you yell at me, or so much as yell at mom, I'll set this this place alight like an alkali with no control."

His dad stepped back as his mom stared, wide-eyed. Pele slammed his door, chucking his phone at his bed. All he freaking wanted was to talk to the *one* person who gave a crap.

* * *

Montana's phone buzzed. She eyed it and picked it up with an eye roll.

"Yeah, I saw they lost, Juana."

"Not that," Juana's dismissed her statement. "Raul said Pele and Jessica had a fight."

"Not surprised." Montana stifled a yawn. "Pele's smart. Jessica's a cold-hearted manipulative snake."

"Well Raul would like you to check on him because he used magic to open the back hall door."

Montana sat up. "What?"

"Yeah, Raul said there was this explosion of light, Pele stormed out, following by Jessica. They fought. Pele left, so if you could..."

"I will, don't worry. I will."

Montana hung up the phone, buzzing with static. She recited her mantra ten times to calm down. Pele rarely used his magic. Even the kids with small amounts would use it now and again. But not Pele. So whatever Jessica had done was way bigger than Montana's tiff with him.

She pulled up her texting app. He hadn't responded. She idly tapped the side of her phone. But no text she tried to compose seemed right. So she called.

It went right to voice mail. Montana took a deep breath.

"Hey Pele, it's Tana. Heard about tonight. I'm sorry. If you need to talk I'm here." She nearly hung up. "Though actually I need to talk to you about something completely unrelated. Anyway, call, text," the answering service beeped, "you know the drill." She sighed and hung up.

Montana tossed and turned. Until somewhere around 1 a.m. her phone buzzed with Pele's tone, *bada-bada-BA-bada-bada*. She nearly dropped the phone and was then blinded by the screen.

/street coffee 8am sat/

/I'll be there/

Montana reset her alarm after responding, so she woke at the same time she would as if she had school, but ditched half her routine. A quick shower, throw on clothing, grab some cash from her school bag, and off to the bus she went.

Pele was exiting Street Coffee when she got there. He had two cups and a bag, but he looked through and past her.

"Hey," she waved.

Pele blinked. "Hot chocolate?" He handed her a cup. "Walk and talk?"

"Sure," she accepted the cocoa, "but only if there's food. I haven't eaten."

"There is," a half smile slowly materialized on his face. He led them across the street to the satellite campus of the

University of Arizona. They walked around the buildings until 7th Street was out of sight. Pele sat on one side of the bench and sighed. Montana sat on the other side. This was probably the first nonschool day they'd ever hung out.

"You okay?" She asked as he handed her a sandwich from the bag and then grabbed one for himself.

He didn't answer right away. And she couldn't read him as well as she used to. She hoped it meant that he'd gotten better at hiding his feelings not that she was losing her touch.

"Yeah," he nodded after finishing his first bite. "Nothing like a little humility to put you back on track."

"Dare I ask?" She watched him as he ate half his sandwich, then finished the second half in one giant bite.

Leaning forward, Pele put his elbows on his knees, and his head in his hands. "I don't even know why I asked her to Homecoming." He looked at Montana. "It was so random, my question. I didn't think she'd say yes. And I, I," he leaned back head tilted, looking at the sky. "I know you can't go to Homecoming because of that twat, but, well, I promised my dad I'd bring a girl to dinner tonight."

"You want me to play Jessica?"

Pele sat up and shot her a horrified look. "No, just be yourself."

Montana snorted a laugh as she licked her fingers and took another sip of hot chocolate. "Are you sure you want that? With how your dad is?"

"I stood up to him last night." Pele's head was again in his hands, elbows on knees.

Montana placed a hand on his back. "And you got away with it?" she whispered.

"Yeah," He turned his head to her, lifting it. "Yeah." He sat up, eyes wide. "I guess I did." He grinned at her. "So dinner, my house, tonight?"

"In my Homecoming dress?"

Pele cocked his head, brows furrowed. "Sure." A slow smile lit his face. "But if I don't recognize you, don't blame me, I barely knew who you were in street clothes."

Montana laughed. "School uniforms leave a lot to be desired."

Pele stood and gathered their trash. He chucked it in a nearby can. Montana sipped her hot chocolate as she fell into step with him.

* * *

Pele enjoyed walking with Montana. They meandered back across 7th Street into his neighborhood. She'd finished her drink by the time they reached Garfield Elementary School. Pele'd gone to kindergarten and first grade here, before transferring to Arizona State Prep. They sat on the swings, rocking and twirling.

They avoided the subject of Jessica; that was too raw. Instead they began exchanging stories from before they became friends. He was fascinated by the way Montana's static would climb the swing chain when she got upset. And not just about things that had happened to her, but things that happened to him, too.

He was watching the last of the static fizzle when she broke the silence that had descended.

"Pele?"

"Yeah." He focused on her face, but she was staring straight ahead.

"What do you know about your pendant? The one your grandfather gave you?"

"My pendant?" His hand went instinctively for it, remembering Jessica's attempt to take it.

"I'm not going to take it." Montana was looking at him now. "It's just," and she took a deep breath and let it out. "It's just Dr. Wolfy says that the Native Americans made pendants for all the magic users."

Pele's hand slowly fell from his pendant as he listened. He was surprised she was still seeing Dr. Wolfy. He'd thought those sessions had ended after middle school.

"He thinks," Montana continued, "that one would help me control my magic. And if he can prove that, then he can propose reformation of the Powercell program. But he's only got until I graduate high school. Cause I'm his *only* 'subject' that hasn't exploded in public yet." Her voice cracked, her tight fists leaking sparks.

"And you won't." Pele countered. "Jessica blew the shock you gave her way out of proportion," his fists began to clench, "and the school overreacted."

"Because I held it." Montana stated, sparks now skittering up the chain. "And I barely held it long enough to get to the static chamber at Banner's."

"So we build you a static chamber, or find a house with one."

Montana laughed, her static skittering away. "Do you have a million dollars, cause I sure don't?"

"Oh," Pele slumped, "but my pendant would work the same?"

"Not yours," Tana half smiled, "one of my own. The paper Dr. Wolfy found focused on how Native Americans used the same arcane symbols as medieval Europe, but there was brief mention that the pendants were used to equalize everyone's powers."

Pele pulled out his pendant. On the front was an upward pointing equilateral triangle, dissected by a horizontal line. On the back his three-year-old self's fingerprint was stained into the wood with remarkable clarity. He glanced at Montana, and pulled his swing closer to hers. Her eyes flicked between him and the pendant.

"Touch it."

"What?" She furrowed her brows at him.

"Touch my pendant."

She reached out like ET and tapped it. He took his hand and flattened hers against it. He felt energized, if anything, certainly not fatigue.

"Try and pull power through it."

"What?" Montana laughed, but he kept her hand there.

"I'm alkali. If alkalis could pull power the world would be dust."

Pele frowned, still trying to figure out why Montana's touch was different. "Try, please."

Montana took a deep breath. There was a slight drain, still no fatigue, though. He couldn't quite place the taste because it was too faint, but it wasn't copper.

"The bitch." Pele let Montana's hand go. She squeaked as they swung apart. "Somehow she knew she could pull my power that way."

"She's metaloid." Montana stopped her swing, facing him. "The first time we met she tried to pull my power after insulting my mom."

"My mom!" Pele jumped off his swing. Thoughts raced

through his head as he headed homeward. "My dad's metaloid," he said, as Montana caught up. "But he's always used alkali earth magic, my mom's magic. What if she can't leave him because he wears her pendant?"

"Then we get it back."

Montana's energy crackled beside him.

* * *

Montana heard the yelling through a kitchen window before they reached Pele's front door. He cringed.

"I gave the boy a list!"

"You can do this," she whispered as Pele hesitated, his hand on the door knob.

He looked back. Montana set her 'I mean business face' and nodded. He set his expression.

"Speak up woman! I can't hear a damn thing you say!"

Pele threw the door open, stepping inside. "Dad!"

He froze. Pele's dad swung toward them. Montana gasped, trying to comprehend the scene before her. She gave Pele a push toward the kitchen as she began her mantra. *Control. That's my desire. Control. To stop my electric fire. Control.*

Pele's mom sat at the table, a knife piercing the table between her ring and middle finger. Pele's dad held the handle. A flash of another man holding a knife to her mom passed through Montana's vision.

"Who the hell's that, boy?" Pele's dad yanked the knife from the table. "She ain't no cheerleader, let alone a lead."

"I ain't dating the head cheerleader anymore, Dad."

"So you found some bum off the street?" The knife pointed at Pele.

Montana's vision focused on it, her dad superimposed on Pele, who raised his hands to show that he wasn't a threat.

Control. That's my desire. Control. To stop my electric fire. Control.

"No!" Montana stepped forward, focusing, focusing all her might to remain contained. "I'm his best friend." She stared Pele's dad down, lightning arcing around her body. "And I want you to give his mom her pendant back."

The man laughed, once. He stepped forward until the knife was centimeters from her throat. "And what are you going to do?"

Montana's body was shaking. Pain building up in her gut. She would stop this, she had control. That knife was metal—lovely conductive metal—and it was so close.

"Tana?" Pele's voice quavered.

Montana brought her hands up, palms facing Pele's dad. As he smirked, she turned them palms facing, sending sparks arcing from her to the knife. Arcing from her to the man. He stumbled into the kitchen counter. The knife clattered to the floor. Pele's mom yelped.

Montana pulled her hands in, clutching her stomach. The world began to twirl. A light exploded. Montana focused on Pele's dad. He clutched a necklace. Montana pulled a hand from her stomach, willing the sparks to stay inside, willing her hand to be clear. The man stayed steady. She reached for the necklace.

"Give it back."

He let her take it. She only touched the string. Rasping for breath, quickly losing energy by trying to control herself, Montana turned. She tossed the pendant and Pele caught it. She reeled into the table, doubling over, clutching the warm wood.

"Tana?"

She pulled out her phone, still trying to keep the static away from the one hand. She called Dr. Wolfy. Even as it rang, she slid it to Pele's mom. She looked into the woman's eyes.

"Get out. Tell Dr. Falkenwolfe what happened, but get out."

"Montana, I am on my vay," Dr. Wolfy answered.

"Take the phone and GET OUT!"

She slid to the floor, curling in on herself. She couldn't let it out. She'd seen what her mom had done. Montana knew that she had only survived because she, too, was alkali. Pain ripped through her insides, from her head to her toes. Copper invaded her mouth. Someone screamed.

* * *

Pele gave his statement to the police, who'd arrived shortly after Dr. Falkenwolfe. The moment the paramedics had whisked his dad away in an ambulance, Pele was at Dr. Falkenwolfe's side, his heart pounding.

"She's alive, isn't she?"

"Yes." The doctor knelt in front of Montana, disregarding the tiny sparks that flew here and there. Sitting back, he let out a deep sigh. "Amazing." A touch of pride colored his Germanic accent. "She internalized it, but," he stroked his chin, "at vat cost?"

He picked up the black rubber-like blanket he'd brought in with him and wrapped Montana in it. Pele felt helpless. His hand clasped his pendant and he remembered their conversation.

"My pendant!" He lifted it over his head. "Maybe it would help."

"Pele!" his mother grabbed his shoulder. "Don't make my mistake."

He looked at her, then to Montana. "But she helped us, Mom. She's been my defender and friend since second grade. I trust her."

"With your life?" his mom whispered, her other hand firmly clenched around her pendant.

"Yes."

Pele placed the pendant over Montana's head and nestled it under the big black wrap. The sparks didn't sting that much. He felt heavy, so he sank down to sit with his back against a scorched table leg. He felt Dr. Falkenwolfe and his mom stare at him. He just needed to sleep.

* * *

"Pele?"

Montana's groggy voice brought Pele back to consciousness.

"Yeah, Tana?"

"Why am I wearing your pendant?"

Before he could answer two shadows appeared in the kitchen doorway. The thin short frame of his mother, and a tall wiry frame that was not his father.

"To save your life," Dr. Falkenwolfe said. "But Mrs. Vindsong has arranged for us to meet a shaman so zat you may have one of your own."

SKINWALKERS

Michelle Schad

A swirl of smoke drifted up from the cigarette held loosely between my fingers. I peered at the sky from the roof of my flat. The rough shingles felt like sandpaper against the soles of my bare feet. A heavy blanket of dark clouds rolled in across the horizon, blotting out the sun as it sank into the mountain. I watched the clouds. They carried an ominous song inside them that made my skin prickle. I cracked my neck in a poor attempt to shake it off. It did no good. Something foul sat heavy on those clouds, weighing them down.

"Something's coming," I said to myself, blowing out a stream of smoke from my nose. I needed to know, needed to see through the veil to be sure. I didn't like what I saw in the clouds, what I smelled in the air. I skipped dinner, feeding off of what Mother Nature could provide instead. My brother would call it psychotic; I called it intuitive nourishment.

As I was about to hop back inside to make preparations for my evening's communion, a boom of thunder announced the coming storm.

Fat droplets of rain collided with the packed earth beneath me. My body rocked back and forth, shivering in the cold. The sound of my heartbeat thrummed deep inside my chest and into my ears, my veins surging with euphoric energy. A chant carried itself up to the full moon that hid behind the blanket of hateful clouds. They carried the first storm of the summer in their thick gray folds. It took several moments before I realized the chant I heard had erupted from my own chest.

The magic of the Earth was all around me. Every rock and tree was illuminated in my vision as a tiny pinpoint of light just as the first crash of lightning struck the ground. I saw the power and spirit within each living thing, saw the gateways and paths to the Otherworld just beyond the veil that divided our world from theirs. I smiled, ready to take my first step along that path, but as I did the scenery shifted.

Instead of bright pinpoints of light, my surroundings shriveled and diminished. Fractals of blue turned blood red. The thunder I heard turned to terrible growls that ripped through me, piercing me with agony. I know I screamed like the Devil had taken me. It was not the first time. I screamed every time the vision shifted, each time hoping I might see something different.

Something in Heavenswood was wrong; a looming threat that would drown our tiny little town. Trouble was, no one believed me.

There was a point in time when the people of Heavenswood would actively seek out my mother, ask her to read the patterns on the wind or reach beyond the veil into the Otherworld for guidance. When she died, folks stopped coming. They mourned with us, but then, eventually, stopped talking to us all together. Then, at some point, they stopped believing.

Gradually, my screams diminished to pathetic gurgles and my chanting to whimpers in the rain. Each fat droplet of water beat against my brow and bare chest. They flooded my nose and ears. I felt myself sinking into the mud that surrounded me. It drew me into its cold embrace until I was one with the Earth.

"...jah! Elijah!"

Light flooded my unfocused eyes. It was painful. I cringed and spluttered, rolling like a beached turtle in a pool of thick muck and castor oil. Every part of me was sore, made worse when my brother pushed repeatedly on my chest. It hurt.

"Jesus Christ, you asshole!" my brother spat. "What the hell is wrong with you! You wanna die too? What'd you take this time!"

The list was too long to give a proper answer, so I opted for silence. I still felt as if I were part of the Earth, my body absorbed into the cold suction of freshly made wallows. An answer wouldn't ease Noah's anger anyway. He didn't believe anymore. I did; I had to. It felt wrong *not* to believe.

"Answer me, dammit!" Noah demanded again. He liked pushing on my chest, which only served to shove me further into the Earth. I felt it ooze into my ears and cradle my neck. I wasn't coherent enough to speak without slurring it all up into a single syllable. I wasn't strong enough to pull free of the Earth, either. Truth be told, I didn't want to.

"God, you are such a waste," Noah cursed. I knew he didn't mean it, but in that moment, it certainly felt like he did. Maybe I was a waste, but I was a waste that was trying to save what he loved so much—the people of Heavenswood. No one believed the town idiot though, no matter how much he might beg or plead to be heard. Rather than argue, I simply lay there in the aftermath of the storm.

I listened to my brother leave. His heavy, squelching footfalls traveled through the ground to the tiny drums inside my ears. When I could no longer detect his presence within the Earth—or any other capacity—I choked through a coughing fit of foul-tasting vomit and dirt. Still, as I lay there recovering coherency, I felt the land around me trying to send out a warning, to tell me what so desperately needed to be known. *They* were coming.

Eventually, I crawled out of the saturated ground, naked to the world, and trudged my way back to the flat above my father's old garage. It was archaic and rickety. The stairs complained in loud creaks and groans as I climbed them. The walls were painted with soot that never washed away after the fire. There was a smell to it, too, that I could never place, but I felt bereft when it was not there.

I washed the memory of my vision away in the shower that only had one pressure setting. I stood there for long minutes, letting the scalding water burn each terrifying vision away until I was able to stand without support. I could hear my mother's sweet voice telling me to hold on to my faith, to listen to the winds for they would guide me when I needed it the most. I wanted to believe her. Belief was hard when I stood alone, and the winds howled in a cacophony of impending chaos.

I can't do this without him. He needs to believe, I thought, hoping my brother might hear.

Our home among the foothills of Heavenswood was small, divided into two different parts. Noah lived in the main house with a large garage a few yards away from it. He was a hard worker, provided for anyone that came across his path and, usually, loved without condition—unless that person was me.

I lived above the old garage in the burnt-out shell of what our lives had been when we were children. The twisted carcass of our father's car still sat in that cruddy garage, weeds and flowers taking over the soot and gravel after the accident that took his life. I tried keeping a job and, technically, had one at the local bar in town, but I wasn't always sober enough to stand up, let alone serve drinks. Herbs and visions aside, I knew my shortcomings. No one really saw the Otherworld high on heroin, but I did that as much as I did peyote herbs.

I knew that's why people refused to believe. I'd done it to myself. Drunk, addict, loser. I wasn't the only one, though. So many of the Seneca drown themselves in liquor or gave in to the drugs that Mother Earth provided—especially the ones still on the reservation. We were just off the reservation—far enough away to prosper, but close enough to still get caught up in their crap.

Long after my shower, I shuffled in to the new garage where my brother worked, my steps echoing. I wore sunglasses and flip-flops beneath ragged jeans and no shirt. I wove my way around the towers of rubber tires that stood as sentinels in the dusty lawn outside. They guarded against the armies of rusted, busted cars that filled five acres worth of crabgrass. The junkyard was one of the few eyesores in the small mountain town, but it was tolerated for the talent that was held within.

Noah hung halfway down into the engine of an old '67 Chevy C10. It was a restoration job for a member of the local sheriff's office. The price tag on the restoration would easily pay the bills and upkeep on the yard for the next three months and then some.

"Lookin' good, Noh."

He shoved himself out of the Chevy with a heavy sigh. Sweat poured down his temples, the bandana that held back his blue-black hair collected what pooled at his ears. Muscular arms twisted his hands into a dirty red rag that I knew he wished could be my neck sometimes. Sometimes I wondered if his life really would be easier without me like he always claimed it would be when he was done with my crap. I answered the question as soon as it hit me, but I wondered all the same.

"It's noon, Eli. Noon. I asked you to come help almost four hours ago when I slapped you out of your drug-induced stupor. You weren't breathing this time, by the way—aiming for a new low?"

I shrugged, lighting up a cigarette. Noah only rolled his eyes at me.

"Why do—"

"I'm doing it again tonight," I cut in. "They're coming. We need to be ready."

"No one is coming, dammnit. No one," he barked. He didn't believe it though; I could see it on his face. He remembered what happened when we were children. We both still had the scars to prove it—his across his face and mine across my stomach. He shook his head, instead, digging around his tools for the item that would help with his current task.

"You need a smaller ratchet," I rasped. Noah had turned away from me, trying to ignore the truth in my words by immersing himself in work. He growled and threw the ratchet he'd picked down into the dirt. I glanced at it through a swirl of smoke that I blew out through my nose toward my angry twin.

Stop fighting, moron. Seriously, when did you stop believing? When Mom died, or when I did?

Noah looked at me sharply then turned to the tool chest that once belonged to our father. Neither one of us liked to talk about what happened when they came the first time. No, that was not entirely true either—they came every thirteen years but, usually, no one noticed. The last time anyone had really noticed was in the fifties when the entire town was nearly wiped out in a single night. The media had called it one of the most gruesome serial killings ever recorded. Newspapers took black-and-white pictures of mutilated corpses and blood-soaked trees; reporters gave their account of things from behind the barrier of caution tape plastered over every door and window. By contrast, the most recent incident had left only four corpses to photograph and two bandaged boys lying in hospital beds. Every single one of those photos were all shoved in a dusty box, an unsolved crime that was easily forgotten.

I wanted to say more, but my attention was diverted by the crunch of gravel. Noah looked at me as soon as he saw the sheriff's car rolling up to the garage but all I could do was shrug. There was nothing illegal about ashes in a conch shell and I was currently devoid of anything more potent than cigarettes and a case of cheap beer.

"Afternoon, gentlemen."

I arched a brow as a woman climbed out of the driver's seat and Steve Lowry climbed out of the passenger's seat. The woman was nearly a match in height to my brother and I, which meant she reached Lowry's shoulders quite easily. She had her hair in a braid that was tucked up into her wide-brimmed hat. It was like she stepped out of a TV show with the get-up she wore, but what got me more was the aura around her. She looked...fuzzy.

"Boys," Lowry said. "This is our new sheriff, Ever Jackson. Y'all got a minute?"

"Wasn't me," I said as I tossed the cigarette to the ground and shuffled back to the house to brew some coffee. Noah only sighed and followed.

"Are you serious?" Noah asked after the new sheriff and Lowry finished their explanation for their visit. The Baxters were a nice old couple that lived on the lake. According to the sheriff, they were having some sort of issue, but the old woman would not talk to anyone except me, of all people. The sheriff made an apologetic face and opened her mouth to speak but I cut her off.

"You're driving and I'm not putting a shirt on."

There was no further discussion, I simply shuffled my way out to the squad car and lit up another cigarette on the way. The ride into town only took fifteen minutes. I rode with the window down, letting the wind hit me in the face and blow through my long hair. When we got to the Baxter home, I tied my long locks back into a messy man-bun and pulled a multi-colored scarf from my back pocket, tying it around my head. I'd worn it the night before and every time

I wanted to touch the Otherworld. My mom had worn it too, when she had done what I do now.

"Mrs. Baxter?" Sheriff Jackson said. Her aura wavered, shifting with a crack in her voice to something more solid. She was hiding something that made me grin a little; a secret she kept just to herself. "Mrs. Baxter, it's Sheriff Jackson. I brought Mr. Curtis with me. Can we please talk now?"

A few minutes passed but, eventually, the door opened. I'd known Mrs. Baxter my whole life. She taught first grade way back when and now enjoyed a retired life with her husband. Every morning, they sat in their rockers, sipping steaming mugs of coffee while watching the comings and goings of a small town. Now, she looked at me with the desperation of a woman at her wit's end.

"Come in," she said. She stood aside as everyone entered, watching everyone carefully. She saw the sheriff's aura, too. I saw the way her gray eyes narrowed with curiosity just like mine had.

The house smelled of mothballs and Dawn dish soap. Mrs. Baxter was seventy, maybe a little older. There were family pictures and afghans and little handmade doilies all over the place, but there was no warmth in the home at all. I rolled my neck uneasily, shivering. Mrs. Baxter looked at me and I felt my breath catch in my chest.

They took him.

"All right, Mrs. Baxter, now, can you tell Mr. Curtis what you won't tell us? We can't help you find your husband until you do."

"You won't find him," I said. Or, rather, I heard myself say. It was like a part of me detached and flew away to the pre-dawn hours at the dock just behind the Baxter's home.

"You won't... Tell her I love her; tell her I love her and to run; tell her... they're coming; they're all coming."

I watched from a distant, hazy vantage point as Mr. Baxter walked onto his dock with a fishing pole and tackle box. It was a morning ritual. Mrs. Baxter wanted trout for dinner and, by golly, he was going to snag her some trout to fry up. She had her reasons and would do some weird voodoo with its guts but that was her way and he was all right with that. I watched him settle into his faded green chair and then felt his pain. I couldn't see anything because, in that moment, I *was* Mr. Baxter. He didn't know how or why, just that he hurt, and *they* were doing it to him; then—nothing. There was no light, no dark, just an incredible amount of pressure that suddenly burst like a bubble when I shot up off Mrs. Baxter's floor like a weed.

"Ok, relax. Breathe slowly. You had some sort of seizure or something," the sheriff was saying, but I knew better. So did Mrs. Baxter. I looked at her and she knew. The tears welled in her eyes. I watched her walk back into her bedroom and come back out a few minutes later with something in her wrinkled hands. She draped a set of quartz and obsidian beads around my neck, nodded, and walked out her back door.

"Mrs. Baxter!" I called. I tried to get up but I was dizzy and tripped. Her house kissed the woods, touched the lake and sky—basically lived on the edge of reality and the Otherworld. "Wait!"

"Mr. Curtis, sit down!" the sheriff called, chasing me as I chased Mrs. Baxter. I made it ten steps out onto her back porch when I caught scent of them; the *tayonih*. The hairs on my neck and arms stood on end and the large tattoo on my back suddenly burned with ferocity. Mrs. Baxter had already gone, willing and ready to join her husband without fear. This was normal for her, this was how it always happened in Heavenswood, and she was ready. She'd met her husband that fateful summer in '51 when everyone else had been killed. She'd left Heavenswood to go to school and was there, studying in the library when her people were slaughtered. She knew. Everyone in town knew even if they'd forgotten. Maybe that's why they were so angry all the time and wanted so much more than life could give them. Everyone had forgotten their faith, their purpose; forgotten.

"Mr. Curtis, please, I'd like for you to go see a doctor," the sheriff said. "Lowry, go find Mrs. Baxter."

"No!" I barked. "Stay out of the woods."

Lowry looked at me then at the sheriff, clearly torn. He was starting to remember, but he had a duty to obey his superior officer.

"Oh, for the love of Christ, someone needs to go find that woman! Stop being such an infant!"

"Lowry, I don't like you," I said with pure honesty in my voice as I stared at the woods. "You were the biggest asshole in high school and still rank high on my list of douche bags. I'm begging you—stay out of the woods."

There was uncomfortable silence from the elder man and then a rough cough as he cleared his throat. "How many?"

"All of them," I said. "We've forgotten."

"Eli, I have little girls, man, they're only two."

"I know."

"Would either of you like to explain to me why you're both staring at a bunch of trees like you've just seen the Devil walk through them?"

I snorted, "Trust me, Ever—may I call you that? Not even the Devil would go in there right now."

I turned around and walked back through the house to the squad car. Lowry and the sheriff followed, arguing with each other the entire time. "I need to go see Blind Jack."

I lit another cigarette as I spoke. I was feeling a little twitchy from all the visions and lack of heroin in my system. It'd been two days since my last hit of that particular poison. I climbed into the back of the squad car and waited.

"This isn't your own personal taxi service," Ever said. "I brought you down here to help me question a witness about a missing person. Now I've got *two* missing people! And now you're telling me you want to go talk to someone else—stop smoking in my squad car!"

She snatched the cigarette from my lips. In that moment, I caught a momentary glimpse of a little boy in a dress with a black eye and bloodied nose, sobbing, not because of the pain, but because the dress was now stained.

So that's your secret...

I looked at her, very calmly got out of the squad car, lit another cigarette, and started walking up the road back into town. Blind Jack lived along the woods too, like the Baxters, just north of my own home. He didn't talk to anyone. He got all that he needed from weekly deliveries that his niece left on his front porch. He was like me, like my mother had been, but grouchy and nasty. The Otherworld had touched him in a horrible way, had taken the light from his soul and turned it dark and ugly.

"Hey!" she shouted. I ignored her. I smoked and walked, glancing at the cats that had run out of Mrs. Baxter's house. They all followed me, all three of them. I smiled at that, wondering what the sheriff might make of them, wondering if she knew what she'd stepped into. I felt bad for her, after a fashion. We were entering the next cycle, and it was going to be an awful one. For her sake, I hope she took the hint and got out of town before things got rough—she seemed like a nice guy.

I pulled my phone out of my pocket as I walked and dialed my brother. It was three miles back to town and then another five to Blind Jack's.

"Curtis Auto," Noah said. I shook my head. Always working, always serious.

"Reina back yet?" I asked.

"Been arrested yet?" he threw back.

"I'm serious, Noah—she back yet?"

"Why do you care? You're not exactly her number-one fan."

I wasn't. To be fair, my brother's girlfriend wasn't exactly *my* biggest fan either. We had a mutual hatred of each other.

"Just tell her to pack Cessa's stuff—they need to leave. I'm going up to see Blind Jack."

"What, why? Elijah, what's going on? Eli—"

I hung up as the sheriff's squad car rolled up beside me. I had faster ways of getting to Blind Jack's and I was tempted to show the sheriff just what that was, but my head was still spinning from all that had already happened. I would need to save my strength and focus for bigger things.

"Mr. Curtis—" Ever started. She spoke from behind the wheel, car still rolling along at a snail's pace to match my own loping speed.

"Eli," I corrected.

"Eli," she adjusted. "Mrs. Baxter went to great lengths to make sure you were there. You very obviously had a close connection to her and, presumably Mr. Baxter as well. I want to bring them both back safely, but I feel like I can't..."

"No, you can't. They're already gone, Ever. The best you can hope for is saving everyone else. You look like a smart woman—I assume you read the town's histories and old case files—we don't have many. Do me a favor and count back... five sets of thirteen years."

"You're talking about the Massacre of '51. Ok, what does that have to do with a crazy couple that just walked off into the woods?"

"They weren't crazy and it's about to happen again."

"What's about to happen again?" she asked. She stopped the car and got out. I kept walking. The cats followed, their tails up in the air as if on alert. They knew. "Eli! Don't think I won't arrest you for ... for..."

"What's your actual name? Did you get Ever from something longer? Everett maybe?"

She stopped walking and stared at my naked back for several minutes before realizing that I'd moved on. She ran to catch me then grabbed my arm to turn me to face her. Again, I caught a glimpse of her past, of a boy sitting on a sofa while an elder man hollered that no son of his would love another man. I looked at her when the glimpse went away, looked at her eyes and saw the weight she carried in her heart clearly displayed in pools of green.

"I like Everett, too," I said and kept walking. "I think I like Ever better. Has a... I dunno... ring to it that Everett doesn't. Everett sounds too boring. Go read those files again, Ever."

"Oh, hell no you are not doing this," she said, running to catch me again. Again, she grabbed my arm and turned me around. This time I saw a man staring at his reflection in the mirror, makeup perfectly done and short hair growing out to tight ringlets that would have to be tamed soon. "Explain yourself."

I blinked and refocused on the sheriff. "Telling you that you're out of your league seems a little cliché, but it is the honest truth. This isn't just a normal small town. There's history here and expectations. People don't like to be reminded of that though. If they're smart, they leave. If not... well, I shouldn't talk. I'm still here, right?"

"You aren't making a single bit of sense and—are you seriously going to walk to wherever you're going?"

"Yeah, it's only eight miles or so back the way we came. I've walked further," I said. I had. "If we survive, wanna have a drink with me?"

"What?" she crowed, totally thrown by my random invitation.

"I'll take that as a maybe," I said, winking at the new sheriff. She made to follow me, but this time Lowry stopped her. I heard him tell her it wasn't worth it, I was a different brand of weird, even for this town. *Ass*.

By the time I made it up to Blind Jack's it was late afternoon and the sun hid behind the canopy of verdure above me. The small shack that the old man lived in looked like it might fall over or just crumble to pieces. The porch creaked and the wind chimes made of bones gave it an eerie look. There was an eerie feel to it too, a smell of death that always lingered.

"Jack?" I knocked. No answer. "Jack, you there?"

I listened instead. He wasn't one to answer if he didn't feel like it. The wind blew through the trees in a soft symphony. The chimes hanging from the eaves clattered together.

The cats that had followed all stayed at the bottom of the hill, all mewling anxiously. Even with the stench of death that surrounded Blind Jack, I could smell them; that same scent that set my hairs standing on end at the Baxter home. It was worse here. My stomach knotted.

"Jack?" I banged on the door this time. The screen recoiled back, rattling. Dust fell off the screen but there was no answer. They'd already been there, I realized. In fact, the *tayonih* were still there. "Shit."

Running did no good, so I just very calmly walked my way back down the hill. Or, as calmly as a knotted stomach and twitchy shoulder blades would allow. At the base of the hill, my passel came to a halt. Ever stood there with the cats circling her feet.

Double shit.

"Do you know that not a single goddamned officer on my squad *actually* knows where Blind Jack lives?" she said to me. "Not one. They just—and I quote—leave the old coot alone."

The smell grew stronger and the tattoo on my back burned something fierce. My skin crawled, needing to shed itself for something else. It would be the only way we might stand a chance. Before, I'd been too young. Now...

"Well, he is known for violent outbursts," I said, hooking my arm through hers. "About that drink. I was thinking now."

"You're certifiable. How high are you right now?" she said. I looked at her. "Oh yeah, I looked at your record, too. Your file is bigger than the files we have for traffic infractions, Mr. Curtis."

"Is it?"

When the burning spread across the whole of my back, I stopped moving. When it shot down my spine, I felt myself go rigid. The cats that had followed from Mrs. Baxter's house hissed and snarled. The wind shifted and the chimes went still. I looked at my chest, at the beads Mrs. Baxter gave me and slipped them off. I put them on Ever instead and shoved her back into her squad car.

"Go to my house. You'll be safer there. Don't ask, just do. Dinner and a drink."

She gave me a look but then blinked, as I knew she would. Her green eyes grew wide with shock, then terror, as my skin peeled away and my form shifted. I became one with the world around me, felt the Earth beneath me and the sky above. From deep inside my chest came a primal roar that was answered by a series of threatening howls. I dropped to the ground as bones cracked and shifted, the sounds around me resounding in my head.

I thought of my brother and his stupid girlfriend. I thought of Cessa, who liked pancakes with sprinkles and was not nearly as stupid as her sister. I thought of Susan and Mike and the countless hours I spent at their bar. I thought of the guitar on my bed and the dreams I'd once had to be a musician instead of a junkie. I thought of the homework for psych class that was due in two hours; I hadn't even started it.

"Holy shit!"

I heard Ever's exclamation, though it was an echo into a mind that thought more clearly and along different patterns than it had mere moments before. I stood in front of the squad car, not as a man, but as a large cat, facing my enemies with idiotic bravado. Emerging from the woods were three wolves as large as the squad car that roared to life behind me.

I was expecting Ever to leave. Instead, my now overly sensitive ears rang with the sound of gunshots. She hit all three wolves square in the chest. Not one to overlook a gift, I took advantage of that shock and attacked the leader. I felt the power of my strike across its face. I felt a carnal need to sink teeth into flesh and tear it apart. I came close, tasting the blood of my enemy on my tongue. They'd been trying to get rid of us for ages. I'd be damned if they succeeded on my watch.

Despite Ever's help, a three-to-one fight was simply not going to go well. The dammed dogs were stronger but I was faster. I lead them on a goose hunt away from Ever and back down the hill. I had the advantage of stalking amongst the trees while they were left to paw at the bark. The closer I got to my home, however, the worse I felt—like a stone of dread that weighed me down.

My nightmares came true when I reached my house ahead of the squad car. I saw my brother beneath one of the wolves, still as death. I don't know that I really thought things through when I jumped on the wretched dog's back. There were three more still coming down the mountain and I got it in my head to attack a fourth.

It cried out as my claws dug into its flesh and rended it apart. We crashed into the tire towers and rusted cars. This one was far bigger than the other three—the alpha. We had no alpha because we had all forgotten. The only ones left were, me, my brother, and Blind Jack—and they'd already gotten Blind Jack. By the looks of my brother, they'd gotten him, too. That meant it was just me, and I was hardly alpha material.

We fought and rolled, the wolf and me. I wondered what nature lovers might make of this fight—a cougar and a wolf the size of small sedans rolling around in a graveyard of old cars and rusted metal skeletons.

I shouldn't have been thinking about things like that. It gave the wolf the advantage. I felt its jaws sink into my shoulder and howled, wrenching myself around and kicking a form that was not quite as natural as it should have been. I embraced what I was, but skinwalking didn't come easy when one was high or drunk or hungover. Either way, I managed to get the wolf off me, knowing it would be mere moments before it gained the upper hand again.

Instead, I got to watch my new crush drive her squad car right into the bastard and crush it against the lift in the garage. I panted, limping toward the garage cautiously in case she'd missed. She hadn't. The bloodied, broken body of a young man was now draped over the hood of her squad car. Perhaps he *wasn't* the alpha. Damn.

"I just killed someone," Ever said as she stumbled out of the car and leaned against it.

"Noah!"

I let a low growl out at Reina as she ran to my brother. He lay in a pool of his own blood, face the color of ash. He was alive—barely. Reina's little sister stood sobbing in the doorway with her stuffed bunny clutched in dirty arms. He'd been trying to protect them.

My concern was broken by a series of howls that tore through the area. Ever moved first, then Reina. They struggled but managed to get my brother inside while I remained outside. I needed to focus and recenter. I needed a warding, something that would give me just a little more time. My attention immediately went to the burned-out garage. Wolves did not like fire.

By the time I got inside, I was covered in dirt, blood, grease, and soot, and wearing a pair of filthy coveralls I found in a box with the top tied around my waist. To my credit, however, I had a wide ring of flames surrounding my house that would burn for a good long while and keep the wolves at bay. It might even turn them away with the amount of vinegar I'd poured everywhere. If we survived, I would have to remember to ask Reina why there was so much vinegar in my garage.

My arm hurt—no, my arm was numb with pain. That seemed impossible but that was the truth. It just hung there, flesh torn where the wolf had bit down on my shoulder. It showed up differently on my skin than it did in my other form. There were other scratches too, claw marks and bites that would linger and bruises that looked black and yellow.

"Noah needs a doctor," Reina said. She had tears rolling down her dark face. I just sighed—we weren't getting out of there any time soon and she knew it. Realistically, my brother would be dead by morning.

"Did he shift?" I asked. She frowned at me.

"What the hell does that—"

"Did he shift?" I repeated with more force. She looked down at him, her face bunching up in pain and disbelief and nodded. I sat on the sofa with my brother and put my hand to his brow. He was cold and clammy, shivering—dying.

Don't give up on me yet, asshole. You don't let me give up on you.

Noah twitched but otherwise didn't move. I looked at the wound and grimaced. It was deep and would be fatal if it was not tended to properly. My fingers absently touched the scar on my stomach, wondering if the *tayonih* were doing this on purpose.

I sighed, looking at Reina, and knew she was entirely useless. The girl just stood there, big amber eyes swollen with tears, hugging herself. I looked at Cessa and saw only fear. I didn't expect much else out of her; she was only seven.

"Hey," I said to Cessa. "Do you know where my private box is in my room? The one you found, and I made you promise to keep secret?" She nodded. "Can you go find it for me now? Please?"

She nodded again and ran off, eager to do anything but stand there and watch her loved ones fall apart. Reina frowned at me and at the sheriff, who still stood there in silent shock.

"Did you just send my little sister to go get you your drug stash?"

"Yeah and I need you to get me some water and find our first aid kit—or tear up some sheets if we don't have a kit in here."

I saw the argument in her amber eyes but shot her a glare of my own that ended the argument before it began. She sneered at me and left to go do what I asked. That left Ever and my brother. I got more discomfort out of feeling Ever's eyes on my back than seeing my brother in the state he was in. I knew this was how he had felt when he'd found me in the same state way back when. Our dad had died protecting us from them back then. They were desperate to be rid of us, to take what they wanted. And they would win now that everyone had forgotten, and the elders were no longer around to keep the peace that ensured another massacre never happened again.

"Ask," I said. I didn't turn around, but the statement was directed at Ever. She flapped her arms at me in exasperation.

"I don't even know where to start."

"We all have our secrets, Ever," I said. "You want to be a girl and I'm really a big cat. Just part of life."

"That is ... did you really just dumb it down to that level?" she said. "There are three *giant* wolves outside! I *watched* you melt into a giant lion!"

"Cougar," I corrected, grinning. Yeah, a cougar was a type of lion if you read its biological break down, but I wasn't going to get into it with her at that moment. It wasn't that important anyway.

I smelled the vinegar and smoke, heard the howls and sensed their presence. It prickled my shoulder blades too much. I *wanted* to run out there and rip them all apart, but I knew I'd never win. It was a primal need that had existed for time eternal. Somehow, I found myself explaining that to Ever.

There had always been skinwalkers who reached through the Otherworld to this one in order to find a new life by taking over early man. There, in our small little town of Heavenswood, we had existed without incident until the massacre of '51. Then, suddenly, there needed to be laws and treaties instead of just loosely respected boundaries. It worked for a while. Those laws were broken thirteen years ago. We were the last of a dying breed, my brother and I. Everyone had forgotten because it was too painful to remember and believe. The *tayonih* had come back to finish the job—and why not? What fight could we possibly put up?

"Everyone in town is like that?" Reina asked. I had not heard her return. She stood with an armful of torn sheets. Cessa had come back, too, sitting beside me with a carved wooden box the size of a small footstool.

"They were at one point," I gruffed. "Most people are still sensitive, though. Why do you think they don't like you? It isn't cuz of your age, Reina—you're one of them. They may not know it, but they feel it."

"Are you shitting me? I cannot—"

"Half-breeds are no less part of the pack," I cut in. "They can smell you for miles—especially when you're in heat."

"You jackass." She tossed the sheets at me and stormed off into the kitchen. I was not the only one in Heavenswood that had a great dislike of my brother's girlfriend. Noah always said it was because folks thought she was too young for him. She was only seventeen and he was twenty-three. Age didn't matter—species did.

"My sister is always horny," Cessa explained to Evar after Reina stormed off. I smiled. I liked Cessa. She was sassy and too smart for seven. She knew what she was and she believed instead of running from it like her sister. It was a shame she wasn't full-blooded or she'd have made a great skinwalker. As it was, she'd make a great seer. She helped me clean Noah's wound and grind the herbs that would prevent infection. She found the little bottles of clear liquids I kept as an emergency stash and watched me inject them into Noah's veins so he wouldn't be in too much pain.

"What's your favorite restaurant?" I asked Ever, turning my attention to the wound on my own arm. There was nothing more I could do for my brother. Ever snorted a dry laugh and shook her head.

"Why?"

"Humor me."

"Cipriano's. It's in the city." She looked at my arm and cleaned the wound. I needed stitches but we had no first aid kit so bandages and duct tape would have to do. "Why do you care so much?"

I shrugged. I didn't want someone from town. I knew them all. It was incestuous and weird. Ever wore a little too much makeup and had an obvious—to me anyway—identity crisis but I wasn't generally too picky, and she was nice besides. I turned into a giant cat and my brother was in a serious relationship with a half-wolf. We had the trifecta of weird in our lives so adding a little more didn't really hurt any.

"You seem nice," I said rather than explain my insane logic. She smiled and even flushed a little. It was cute.

At that moment, the snarls and howls outside my house grew louder. I heard hissing from the cats that had stayed on the porch, a warning that my wards were not going to hold until morning like I had hoped. Reina came back into the living room, walking backwards from the kitchen with a bottle of whiskey in her hand.

"They're kicking dirt up onto the fire," she said breathlessly. "What the hell do they want?"

"Us," I said easily. "We're it. I'm it, really. Noah isn't a threat to them anymore."

"Why?" she cried softly. I shrugged. Why not? Wars had been fought for less among men for centuries. We had a lake full of fish and a forest full of good hunting on a ley line. Skinwalkers literally killed for places like this. The wolves were succeeding. Or so I thought.

We all flinched when we heard the echoing clap of shotguns ringing out into the night. Six shots in rapid succession that could not have possibly come from the same gun.

"..riff...opy?"

Ever fumbled for her radio, trying to find the right signal. Not that it was very strong at my house—we barely managed to get cable television. We had to go into town to watch anything decent.

"This is Sheriff Jackson; Lowry, is that you?"

"...riff...you...y"

"Lowry?"

There was another rain of bullets answered by snarls and growls, whimpers and howls. We heard screaming from those that were attacked. I stood to join them but Cessa stopped me, shaking her head. I dropped back down to her level and smiled.

"I have to go, princess. It isn't fair for them to fight for us without help. Take care of Noah for me, ok?"

She nodded. I looked at Ever, who had the same look of desperation in her green eyes. She didn't want me to go, and that made me feel a little better.

"Cipriano's, huh?" I said in more of a statement than a question. She smiled. I couldn't afford Ciprianos. "How 'bout we start with Denny's and work our way up to Cipriano's?"

"Deal," she chuckled.

I walked out my front door after a stern look at Reina. She knew what she had to do. There were guns in the house, things she could use to defend my brother and her little sister. By the time I hit my porch, I'd shed the man and become the animal. To my surprise, there were three more of my kind waiting for me. They had remembered.

Dawn crept up over the edge of the horizon with the fires around my house burning to mere embers. Two of us remained, plus five police officers, including Ever and Lowry, and a handful of townsfolk that had come up with shotguns and rifles. Old Man Howard even brought up a pitchfork. Seven wolves were littered across my junk yard, their forms reverted back to the men they had been.

The muscles that had been fueled by adrenaline now withered with exhaustion. Pain radiated across my shoulder. I could still smell the *tayonih* on the air, though there were considerably fewer than there had been a few hours ago. This was not over by any stretch of the word, but it was coming to a draw. At least for the time being. We all knew it, too, as we waited in my front yard with solid grips on weapons or twitching tails. The tension still hung in the air. There was concern that this was not the only place where a battle had been fought. Everyone waited for the next round, for the peace to shatter once again. The click of guns being cocked and the growls of large cats echoed across the junkyard when one of the larger wolves stepped forward.

Its fur was grayed with age, but in a way that gave it a sense of wisdom. A large scar ran across its left eye. The other eye was a golden-brown that saw clear through to anyone's soul. I didn't want to look at that eye, but I felt like it was my responsibility to be the one to face this wolf. I stepped forward. Alpha by default.

I See you, mosi. The voice I heard was decidedly female. Not sure why that surprised me, but it did.

I See you. I opted not to add a title; no sense pissing her off more. I already felt my lips curl back from sharp teeth and I yearned to taste more blood. I couldn't afford another fight. I would never walk away from it. She stared at me, studied me, and let out a low growl. And then, just like that, she barked and turned back around. The others followed without question, dragging their dead with them.

"Are they leaving?" Ever asked, her voice no louder than a whisper. I had no way to respond to her. I wasn't ready to let the beast go, not yet. It felt like a charade. I didn't want to trust that what I saw was truth. *Tayonih* would not give up that easily. Why would they? The questions and doubt pounded my head. At that moment however, that was what I had—doubt.

I felt the fur shed off me, the bones crack and shrink as I lost control of my alternate form. My bare back hit the gravel-pitted ground a few minutes later, my ears ringing. Time slowed around me. I felt each granule of dirt and rock beneath me, the tiny pebbles scraping.

Had we really won?

"Eli?"

Ever spoke to me. I was aware of her on the periphery. My eyes remained focused on the sky above. I had no energy left to move them. Her voice sounded distant to me, overpowered by the continual ringing in my ears. I felt a deep throbbing at my side and across my chest. There was a heaviness that settled around me and blurred my vision until tears rolled out of the edges of my eyes. I felt them pool in my ears and finally gave in to the weight around me.

It is an odd thing to watch the chaos of panic from an outsider's perspective, but that was exactly what happened, just as I knew it would. I had no fear of the Otherworld. I walked through it too regularly to fear it. I had no fear of death because we were intimate lovers, constantly courting each other. No one else knew that, though. They screamed my name, pounded on my chest, or just clung to each other and waited until the EMTs could get to me; *if* they got to me.

Things in the Otherworld were different. Colors were brighter in some points, duller in others. Sounds from the real world did not quite reach through that veil that separated the two realities, but the one crystal-clear thing that was always heard in the Otherworld was the sound of running water. Not like a shower or waterfall, but a gentle bubbling like that of a creek moving downstream.

I turned to face the creek behind me. Charon waited, as he always did. I nodded to him and he nodded back. I'd stood on these shores countless times from my own stupidity.

"Well, well," came a tantalizingly husky voice. "Elijah Curtis, son of Noelle; daughter of Omar. Back to Charon's shores already?"

I bowed to the woman that spoke. She was never the same twice, ever changing. Death. It was not my time, not yet, but she courted me anyway.

It never ceased to amaze me how little we actually knew of the Otherworld. Men fought wars over the right and wrong of their beliefs, hated their neighbor over the pendant on their neck. It was all the same; all of it. The power and presence of the Otherworld was pervasive in every aspect of life and death, every blade of grass and tiny rock.

"You come here too often," she continued. "Too often without guidance. Why?"

I shrugged. I didn't have a good enough answer. "Because I'm a jerk heroin junkie" just seemed a little ... flat.

"Is he here?" I asked. She smirked, her dark full lips curved in a predatory smile.

"There is a price to pay for all things in the Otherworld, Elijah Curtis, especially for Bast's children."

"Has he crossed over yet?" I persisted. She smiled,

reaching for my face. Dark fingers caressed my cheek. The scent of her was overwhelming—ginger and dried grass on a damp night. She wore a gown of blood red that simply draped over her perfect form and had bangles of gold at her neck and wrists. They shimmered in a light that was neither bright nor dark.

"Will you give payment?" she purred in my ear. I swallowed hard against the sensation it sent down my spine and let out a slow breath.

"Yes," I whispered. It wouldn't be the first time I'd struck a deal with spirits of the Otherworld. I did what needed to be done. I was known to them.

She smiled, her hand on my bare shoulder now. Her long fingernails were lacquered in black, filed to a point that dug into my flesh and then ripped into the muscle with a swift, precise motion, drawing my heart into her hand. I cried out, dropping to my knees, watching from above where I would be for the next year, a prisoner to the demons of the Otherworld.

On the sofa, in my living room, beneath a pile of blood-soaked rags, my brother gasped with renewed life.

ABOUT THE AUTHORS

S. M. Hillman is a writer, game designer, and freelance game journalist raising his little hatchling alongside his partner and a surly cat. He believes that he has the best family and friends one can buy with his mediocre writing skills and willingness to be a game master for any role-playing game at any time.

L. N. Hunter is a fledgling author, with published work in *Trickster's Treats*, *Rosette Maleficarum*, and *Machine*. L. N. lives in rural Cambridgeshire, UK, sharing a disorganized home with two cats and a soulmate.

Jen Sexton-Riley is a 2018 graduate of Clarion West Writers Workshop and a member of the Science Fiction and Fantasy Writers of America (SFWA). Her short fiction has appeared in *Daily Science Fiction*, *The Colored Lens*, and *Bewildering Stories*, and will appear in 2020 in *Ghostlight: The Magazine of Terror*. She is a staff writer and proofreader at a weekly indie newspaper.

Kathrine Stewart is a lover of all things magical. She lives on the island of Jersey and spends her spare time scribbling stories about fantastical characters and places. She has a number of manuscripts on the go and hopes one day to see her name on the front cover of a book.

Kelsey Wheaton is a short-story author and aspiring novelist, with work appearing in fan-published zines such as *Orion* and *Written in the Stars*. When not obsessing over Netflix reboots of '80s cartoons, she can be found teaching middle-school English.

Karen Garvin has a master's degree in history and writes on a wide range of historical topics as well as writing fiction, which includes short stories and her novel *Seacombe Island*. She is a Steampunk aficionado and avid Victorianist, with one foot in the nineteenth century and one in the twenty-first century. Forget the flying car; where's her airship?

Cathryn Leigh manages the quality aspects of a clinical laboratory by day and experiments with yarn, fabric, and words by night. She's also a wife and the mother of two active middle schoolers, so unfortunately her time for experiments is limited. This year marks the publication of her fourth short story published by Corrugated Sky, and her debut novel, *Love Lost*.

Michelle Schad is a short-story author and novelist. She has work appearing in online fiction magazines, anthologies, and has several novels—with more to come. When not entertaining others with words, she is a tamer of chaos created by her husband, four children, and too many pets.

You might also enjoy

Tales of the Black Dog
Sightings of black dogs go back for centuries and are found in the folklore of many cultures from around the world. In some legends the dogs are harbingers of death, while in others they are protectors. These four short stories provide a modern take on an ancient legend.

Smoke and Steam
These four Steampunk novellas, including "Wings over Staria," "Hekatite," "Heart of the Matter," and "Freedom for a Foster" transport readers to steam-powered worlds where mechanical wings, magic, and supernatural powers rule the day.

Cold as Death
With the release of George Romero's *Night of the Living Dead* zombies shuffled into our nightmares and haven't left. From zombies in space to zombies in the water, these four tales feature the shufflers, shamblers, and brain-munching walkers we all know and love.

Seacombe Island
After a devastating fire, Thomas Ashton flees London for Seacombe Island, where he's swept into a web of deceit involving a volatile energy source refined from the native Hekate orchid. When his new friends are attacked one by one, Tom has to get off Seacombe Island before it is too late.

Hellfire
The United States is a land of opportunity—unless you happen to be "different." Hadi Shahir is different in more ways than one: he's Evolved, and can manipulate fire. When a rash of deadly fires break out in Chicago, suspicion falls on Hadi, whose quiet life gets turned upside down.

Giant Killer Bats of Alamogordo
Ray Riggs and his new bride Sally are travelling across country when a breakdown brings them to the sleepy little town of Alamogordo, New Mexico. They quickly discover something is amiss in the picturesque desert when a huge hunk of meat drops from the sky.

Love Lost
Alethea, destined to become an initiate *mediki*, sets out for the Holy City with Erasmus, who's been tasked with protecting her. Alethea needs to prove that she is not a Dark One, and is worthy of the Lord of Light. But first, she and Erasmus must survive a perilous sea crossing.

Visit us at **www.corrugatedsky.com/** and sign up for our Twitter feed **@corrugatedsky** to stay connected. Be sure to like us on Facebook.

CPSIA information can be obtained
at www.ICGtesting.com
Printed in the USA
FSHW011819121019
62964FS

9 781950 903108